Baby's First Book of Seriously Fucked-up Shit

Robert Devereaux

deadite
press

DEADITE PRESS
205 NE BRYANT
PORTLAND, OR 97211
www.DEADITEPRESS.com

AN ERASERHEAD PRESS COMPANY
www.ERASERHEADPRESS.com

ISBN: 1-936383-50-0

"Showdown at Stinking Springs" originally appeared in Hustler Fantasies.
"Clap If You Believe" originally appeared in Crank.
"Ridi Bobo" originally appeared in Weird Tales.
"Li'l Miss Ultrasound" originally appeared in Gathering the Bones.
"Bucky Goes to Church" originally appeared in MetaHorror.
"Fructus in Eden" originally appeared in Pulphouse.
"One Flesh: A Cautionary Tale" originally appeared in Iniquities.
"The Slobbering Tongue That Ate the Frightfully Huge Woman" originally appeared in It Came from the Drive-In.
"Holy Fast, Holy Feast" originally appeared in Mondo Zombie.

Cover art copyright © 2011 Sebastien Grenier
www.SEBASTIEN-GRENIER.com

Printed in the USA.

OTHER BOOKS BY ROBERT DEVEREAUX
Deadweight
Walking Wounded
Santa Steps Out
Santa Claus Conquers the Homophobes
Caliban and Other Tales
A Flight of Storks and Angels
Slaughterhouse High

To the creative spirit in us all.

Our damnation if we ignore it,
Our salvation if we embrace, nurture,
And set it free to dance
Beneath sun and stars.

Away with all bushel baskets!

CONTENTS

SHOWDOWN AT STINKING SPRINGS

Tiffany knocked. She heard someone—her subject, she guessed, though the step seemed too spry—approach the door and snap open the locks. The ornate brass doorknob eased about.

Kyle Hardwick's weather-beaten face caught Tiffany by surprise, it glowed so with life. More like a horny teenager's, those eyes of his, than a man about to celebrate his hundred and twentieth year. His skin was cracked and scored like old parchment. Some boyhood disfigurement had marked the flesh from his nose to the shell-curve of his ears, as if a shockwave of some sort had blasted it.

"By my reckoning, you'd be the lovely Miss Walker, oral historian *extraordinaire*," he said in tones rich with the sounds of sagebrush and rawhide.

His eyes danced like campfires, his voice as thick and downhome as hickory smoke. Kyle's face, she thought, might even be considered handsome in a perverse geriatric way. A thrill coursed through her. If his memories and the telling of them lived up to this preamble, she might come away with not just something for her archives but an honest-to-God spoken-word recording. She might even spark the interest of a documentarian, a pro like Chip Kendall, whom she had met and bedded in Waco at a conference the summer before.

"I like your apartment, Mr. Hardwick."

He dismissed it with a gesture. "It serves. Live long enough, one apartment's like the next. Won't you kindly take a seat here by the window? Gives you a choice view of the traffic down below. You can set your player on this footstool. Outlet's over yonder."

"Thanks, Mr. Hardwick."

"Welcome. And call me Kyle. All my woman friends do. Got lots of 'em, I do, sweet Tiffany, but there's always room for another. Particularly one with a saucy rump like yours, thighs just made for a man's caress, and a bosom anyone'd be proud to tongue to two stiff blushing points."

Tiffany, taken aback, was more amused than shocked. She put on mock-anger. "Why, sir, you'd best mind your manners."

"Sense of humor. I like that." His eyes twinkled. "Us old codgers, we're as cute and cuddly as snug buttons. Don't go denying it. It lets us get away with talking like that, 'cause we don't have time to waste skirting around the truth. The truth is, I want you Tiffany Walker, and I mean to have you."

She laughed at the audacity of it. Even so, she felt a rush overwhelm her womanhood, moisten it, make it swell in a way she thought absurd. "Well, Kyle, let's get to the business at hand, shall we? You promised"—(here she pressed Record)—"as the sole survivor of the fire that destroyed the town of Stinking Springs, New Mexico, summer of 1882, to relate exactly what happened that day."

"That I did."

He gave Tiffany a wry wink, leaned forward on the sofa, gnarled hands knuckled between his knees, and launched into his narrative.

Everyone, began Kyle, has heard of Paul Bunyan, who scooped out the Great Lakes to quench the thirst of Babe, his big blue ox. And they've heard of Pecos Bill, raised by coyotes, a fellow they say threw fistfuls of fishhooks into his liquor to give it that extra zing.

But few know anything about Hefty Jake Gentry, the hardest-humping, biggest-balled, thickest-dicked darling of all of Western womanhood at the time whereof I speak. And fewer still have heard of Lily Mae Dalton, captured while yet a virgin by a band of Mimbres Apache warriors

10

gone dishonorable, compelled thereafter into a savage love of manflesh, but freed by her own burgeoning appetites. Those braves could break the wildest mustang that bucked and weaved beneath them, but they were no match for Lily Mae when she threw off the shackles of civilized behavior and let free the fire in her belly. To speak plain, she fucked those boys to death she did. When the dust had cleared and Lily gentled her sweat-soaked body down from the heights of orgasm, she was amazed and dismayed to find dead red corpses sprawled everywhere, young and muscular and grinning to beat the band, but dead as dead could be. What was worse to Lily, not yet quite fulfilled, was that their dark dicks hung limp between their thighs, never to stiffen nor thrust again.

From the latter part of the '70s up to their demise on the main street of Stinking Springs in '82, Hefty Jake Gentry and Lily Mae Dalton proved the bane of tiny towns struggling to poke their heads above soil and sprout into bigger ones.

Hefty Jake would ride into town, his pecker as proud and tall as a flagpole behind his saddlehorn, and all the womenfolk'd swarm into the streets, their fingers flying this way and that, tearing off dresses and underthings and flinging themselves down, open and ready, onto billows of muslin and calico. A great keening would fly up into the sky from scores of needy mouths. White arms were flung wide to welcome him in, and whiter thighs as well. The menfolk? They just stood by drained and helpless while virile Jake strode and poked, stroked and sucked, tilled and plowed and Johnny-Appleseeded his way up and down the street. The foolhardy soul who dared go for his gun took one bullet betwixt the eyes and another through the groin for his pains, but Hefty Jake never missed a stroke as he gunned those crazy cockwielders down. Trouble was, the ladies ended up being sated a lifetime's worth. And the men? They were unable to get their dicks up thereafter no matter what the temptation, so demoralizing had it been to watch Jake please their women.

Lily Mae had much the same effect. She went through lovers like a thresher through wheat. And when Lily Mae spent a man, his balls shriveled up tight as two sun-dried peas and stayed that way. His dicktip—though he had to lift the limp thing to see it—wore a thin smile, but it was a smile that said, "I am finished. Wiped out. Done. Fucked and richly paid," not "That was heavenly. Now find me some other woman, cause I'm stiff and ready to slide on home again."

It's a fact of life: Towns die if folks don't fuck new babies into the world.

Towns died then. Lots of them.

Men lost their oomph. Homesteads went undefended, cattle roamed unherded, women were carried off or got fed up at the cockless ways of the demoralized scruffbuckets around them and left. The men sat in saloons listening to off-key piano music and staring at beer. Their minds did nothing but replay memories of Lily Mae straddling them, her wild-honey sex hair swirling up and whipping about like a rage of flame betwixt their belly and hers.

"Seems to be a sheen of perspiration on your brow, Tiffany darling," came Kyle's leathery voice, full of kindness and caring. "Highly becoming of course. Makes your lovely face glow. But maybe you could do with some iced tea or a cool sip of cream soda."

Tiffany blinked in confusion, then pulled herself together. "Um . . . iced tea sounds good." She reached out, hit Pause, and swept a strand of hair into place. Her hands wandered to her lapels. "Do you mind if I—"

"Remove your suit-jacket? Be my guest. You'll be cooler. More comfortable. Besides, it'll give old Kyle a better view of those lovely breasts of yours."

Before Tiffany could reply, he was gone. The bounce in his step astounded her, a man his age. And she could scarcely believe how moist she had grown. It felt good, very good. But ridiculous too. She never went for old men, even ones that came on to her. But Kyle wasn't like them. He was kind and sweet and gentle, despite the frank language of his recollections. His voice was rich and vigorous and, she had to admit it, downright seductive. His hands moved as he spoke, molding his tale as a potter molds clay. The sight of them thrilled her. Those hands had been places, secret places on a woman's body, and they knew how to make those places sing. Kyle returned from the kitchen with a tall tumbler, swirling and clinking with ice. He set it down beside Tiffany's tape recorder and gazed in admiration at the fullness of her breasts. "Beautiful," he said, smiling into her eyes. She struggled for breath. "Nature's bounty," she joked. "They are indeed," he said. His voice, close now, no more than three feet away, rode like a caring lover's tongue up along Tiffany's swollen pussy-lips, pulsing at her clit. She gasped for breath, struggling to hide his effect on her. "Now then," he said, releasing the Pause button and resuming his seat on the sofa, "where did I leave off? Ah, yes."

Right around the time El Paso's famed marshall Dallas Stoudenmire got himself killed on the streets of that fair city, Lily Mae Dalton and Hefty Jake Gentry converged—from opposite ways and unbeknownst to one another—on the unsuspecting town of Stinking Springs, New Mexico.

Town? Hell, it was more like two bricks and a board, a few bent nails, some windows, and a whole heap of prayer and pretending. But back then I called it home, me all of eighteen and knowing no better.

I knew one thing though: My dick was dying to jilt my fist, to wrap itself snug and warm in some gal's wet hot pussy. My friends' dicks too. We pooled our meager funds and drew straws. I won the draw. Went right over to Hank Plowright's smithy, two doors down from the saloon, where he was stoking the fires, preparatory to shoeing a horse. I held out my coins and a grimace broke over his big beefy face. "She's up those stairs, boy," he said. "This buys you fifteen minutes. No more. If your skinny little pecker ain't disengaged from my daughter's twat in fifteen minutes, I'll double-brand your balls, so help me God. Now git!"

I got.

Not two minutes later, Annie and me were free of all fetter and jouncing the fuck out of her springs (they'd suffered a load of jouncing) right there on her mung-stenched bed by a wide-open window that let out onto the main street. Many's the time me and my friends'd loiter beneath that window, listening to some cowpoke grunt his wages into good old Annie Plowright, blazing a trail to heaven. Now 'twas *me* that clambered up her cumulus flesh, hand over fist, approaching the pearly gates of here-I-come-Jesus.

But over the noise of our jouncing, I heard Stinking Springs leap suddenly to life. Doors slammed, dogs took to howling like coyotes, boots pounded on the planking down below, and voices rose up in holler and shout. Couldn't say at first whether 'twas anger, or joy, or fear, or something else that provoked it.

Annie heard it too. She slowed her hips and hove her eyes toward the window. "What the heck's goin' on out there?" she asked.

I told her I didn't know. Didn't much care one way or the other. Not where I was situated at the moment.

"Can the crap, Kyle," she said. "*I* care what's raising such a ruckus. Pull out and let me up."

I did and damned if she didn't lean on the sill, poke her head out the window, reach behind her, and shove my stiffness back up inside her like she was a bitch and I was her spry old hound dog. Felt good to ease into her again and lean down along her back, gathering those big balloony bazooms into my hands. Her hair, which was the color and consistency of straw, smelled like a hayloft, but I nuzzled her neck anyway and found a pleasing rhythm below.

I could see just about the whole stretch of street and most of the buildings over yonder. Folks were lined up three-deep in front of the bank and off in either direction. Faces filled the windows. I thought to pull back for modesty's sake, but no one was taking any notice of Annie and me. They had their sights trained in one direction or the other. What struck me as odd though was that, without exception, the women were staring off to our left and the men sharp right.

The doorbell rang.

Kyle looked up, smiled at Tiffany, and hit the Pause button. "Must be Dawn and Felicity," said Kyle. "Always forgetting their keys. 'Scuse me a second, lovely lady." He rose and went to the door.

Tiffany took the opportunity to kick off her shoes and undo the top buttons of her blouse. She found the old man's voice surprisingly seductive, and its effect seemed to be cumulative: He looked better with each passing moment. She couldn't remember being so horny.

The door burst open under Kyle's hand and two women loaded down with bags of groceries rode the explosion in. They planted wide-mouthed burrowing kisses on his cheeks, kisses that left bright crimson smears. Then they breezed by him, chattering nonstop, into the kitchen. The brunette (Felicity she guessed), tall, lithe, and taut-muscled, sizzled with spring-loaded zest. Her companion, Dawn, was a billowy blonde, as buxom and luscious as a peach tree plumped up and brimming with sun-blushed fruit.

Kyle shrugged happily. "My live-in lovers," he said, resuming his seat. "They may wander in and out. Pay them no mind. They've been told not to bother us."

"Your live-in *what?*"

Dawn poked her head around the kitchen door. "Kyle honey . . . oh, hi . . . um, sorry, Miss—"

"Tiffany," she said. "Tiffany Walker."

"Oh sure, now I remember. Like Tiffany lamps. You look swell. Soft as a peach. Kyle sure can pick 'em, can't he?" Then to Kyle: "You want something to eat, baby?"

"You and Felicity," said Kyle, "I want your sweet tangy nectar oozing all over my face and delighting this old man's tongue."

Dawn beamed a smile that could melt diamonds. "Ooh Kyle honey, you're making me flush and pucker all over." She blew him a kiss and was gone.

"Now where were we?" Kyle asked. "Tiffany?"

She was feeling light-headed. "Um?"

"Undo one more button, will you? For my sake."

She did as he asked.

Kyle smiled and fingered Pause again.

15

***

With my rod tucked snug inside Annie and my palms to either side of her elbows on the window sill, I could see Hefty Jake riding into town off to our left, his jet-black stallion snorting like a raging bull. Jake's manhood rode before him, standing up stiff as a knight's lance. Its tip glistened like red brass in the sunlight and its shaft was as hard and empurpled as dark amethyst.

At the peal of a high whinny to my right, I swung my head about and took in, not far distant, Lily Mae astride a milk-white filly, its chestnut mane flowing free. Jesus God I just about let fly with Old Faithful then and there. Annie was dull meat beside this vision. Lily Mae rode in without a stitch, high-breasted, full-hipped, with a face that begged to be fucked and loved, and hair that tumbled long and blond down her back. Her black leather saddle, studded all over with silver, glistened where her pussy-lips kissed it. Lily Mae dismounted. The sight of her shapely legs and the gape of her golden-haired gash made my heart clamor and half the town gasp. She dropped to the street like a gymnast coming off the parallel bars.

Touching boot to ground, Hefty Jake slapped his steed smack on its ebony rump to give himself room. Then he tore off his clothes and flung them aside. I saw Sadie Flynn the preacher's wife faint and fall in front of the bank. No one noticed her but me, they were all so busy goggling their eyes. You could tell Jake was riled and upset. Put off his stride. He wasn't used to streets that stayed empty of womenfolk this long.

My cock was suddenly awash in whorish cunt-fluid. "Glory be, what a man!" gushed Annie.

"Lily Mae Dalton," shouted Jake. "You plant your pert little butt right back on that filly and ride out the way you came. This town belongs to me."

Her voice shot back smooth as silk, filling the air like the aroma of angel-pussy. "Tell you what, Hefty Jake. I'll hump you for it. First one what makes their offering to the God o' Love skedaddles on out of here and leaves Stinking Springs to the other."

"You're on, gal," he replied. "Bring that gilded twat of yours over here. Let's see what you got."

"Meet you halfway," she said, and the face-off began.

You could feel the air compress and ripple between them as they drew closer—Hefty Jake tanned and muscled, his pecker swaying like an ancient oak in a high wind as he walked; Lily Mae with breasts that jutted and hung, a tight flat plane of belly, hips that flared like nasty tempers, and a pussy that was pure invitation. A water trough began to bubble as Jake strode past it. Then it broke into a full boil, steam rising up from its troubled surface. Two tumbleweeds skittered into one another just behind where Lily Mae's heel detonated a puff of dust. They burst into flame, flared and crackled, and hissed out.

When Jake grabbed hold of Lily Mae's right hip and her fingers closed about his shaft, a whipped-up gust of wind dusted the citizenry. It shoved them back against buildings, brought their hands to their mouths. The wind hit me and Annie as well, gale force. It made it hard to breathe. Hard to keep my eyes open. Behind us, combs and bottles clattered off Annie's dresser to the floor. But I kept stoking her hole, and both of us let our fears fuel our fucking. It was sweet, I'll tell you. Sweet as it gets.

If you've ever seen a skilled artisan daub paint on canvas or turn a pot on a wheel, that'll give you an idea what it was like watching these two legendary lovers have at each other. Foreplay and fondlement at once tender and rough, full of fire and ice, imbued with all the love one sex is capable of feeling for the other and all the scorn as well—that's what blessed my eyes. Like an apprentice doing his level best to ape his master's nimble movements, I tried to mirror Jake's dancing fingers. After a fumble or two, it was clear from the way Annie moaned and groaned that my efforts were paying off.

During this segment of Kyle's narrative, Dawn and Felicity had passed through the living room to the hall at Tiffany's back, on their way to the bedroom, she supposed. Dawn lingered to stare at Kyle, listening rapt and tapping an index finger against her lips. But Felicity coaxed her out of the room

17

and glanced an apology at Tiffany, who waved it off good-naturedly and wondered when Kyle would finish so she could jump his bones.

Now a door opened behind her and the voices of Kyle's two fuckmates danced in her ear.

"Dawn, can't you wait? They won't be long."

"It's okay. We can do him while he talks."

Kyle stroked his chin and sighed at Tiffany. He radiated a patriarch's wisdom, she thought, and the sweet sensuality of youth. "You don't mind, do you," he said, "if I indulge their whims? They're used to being taken care of the instant they get home."

When she had first entered Kyle's apartment, the very idea would have outraged her, made her march right back out again. But she was deep in Kyle's world now, deep in the magic of his voice, deep in what felt, as incredible as it seemed, like love. What he now proposed sounded as natural as breathing. "Yes . . . yes, that's fine."

"Come on in, girls." Then, to her: "Tiffany, would you kindly remove your skirt and blouse?"

She rose to obey as Dawn and Felicity swirled over to the sofa and eased down on either side of Kyle. Felicity looked statuesque in her black bodybriefer, lace with a see-through mesh front. Dawn's aroused nipples pressed forward into a red charmeuse tank top. She had left the panties off and her creamy thighs scissored smooth and lovely as she walked. Laughing, they stripped Kyle where he sat. Then, kneeling on the sofa to either side of him, they bent to mouth him.

Tiffany, in bra and panties—plain cotton underthings she now felt mildly ashamed of—sat down, woozy from the turn-on and finding it hard to swallow. Kyle's gorgeous cock, bowing this way and that like a polite courtier as the women tongued its knobby head, made her cunt muscles flex with hunger. Her idle fingers, gentling along the outlines of her furrow, touched damp cotton.

Kyle reached toward the tape recorder. "One more bit left to my story, Tiffany. Then you can join us."

"Yes, Kyle. I'd like that. Hurry, please. Please hurry."

18

***

Well sir, Jake and Lily Mae grappled with one another that day in the dusty street. And somehow, even though the winds whipped up again and got worse, much worse, I could see them going at it plain as day. Free-swinging signs banged about like blasts of thunder. When Jake shoved a few fingers inside Lily Mae, the sign for Phelps' Feed & Grain tore clean off its hinges and crashed to the planking below, nearly shattering the toebones of my old schoolmarm Miss Pritchard. And when Lily Mae took a good long suck on Jake's dick, the buckboard belonging to the sheriff burst into flame and that flame whooshed onto the tail of the old swayback that pulled it. Poor doomed nag galloped hellbent out of town like a stud in heat.

Tearing off like that more'n likely prolonged the beast's life a tiny bit, because just then Jake and his nemesis joined up genitals, sweet as you please. When that happened, the earth gaped open right in front of the bank and swallowed a whole row of horses tethered to the hitching post. One moment they were standing there, dumb as clothesracks, on solid ground. The next, down they slid into a chasm, legs flailing, necks straining, their eyes wide with terror, their tethers snapping from the dropped weight of them. The earth whomped shut, crushing a terrible waste of good horseflesh in one thin vertical grave, a grave that gushed thick ribbons of blood and lay shut then beneath a shimmering puddle of red.

Despite the quaking of the building we were in, I kept on mimicking Jake, and Annie was lost in shudders of joy at what I was doing. Then, twin telltale groans rose up from the street, getting-ready huffings and puffings that issued from both their throats. At each rising moan, the wind racheted upward a few notches. Chickens went fluttering by the window; small dogs; a babe out of arms. Skirts flared up, handkerchiefs flew to faces, but still the townsfolk squinted through their dust-battered eyelids at the copulating desperadoes.

Then orgasm hit the onlookers. Orgasm hit me and Annie. Hell, orgasm hit the whole godforsaken town. Tops of buildings burst open and geysered their contents into the sky. Bank over yonder became one great spurt of paper money mixed with spangles of gold coin, like tight sperm spinning its way through seminal fluid. But no one had a chance to scoop up any of that money, because just when it reached its high point, the fireball hit. I was watching Jake—I was *one* with Jake doing Lily Mae—so I know where that fireball originated. The two of them were gripping each other hard. Their heads swelled up reddish purple trying to keep from being the first one over the edge. Then they reached that divine inflection point together, eye to eye at last. But it was too late to let it out, because their bodies burst asunder and the fire of their passion flew in all directions. Townsfolk were incinerated like bugs under a blowtorch. A great wave of flame washed up against the buildings like the pounding shudder of a hundred-foot breaker at the beach. Orange engulfment raced up toward us. At the last moment, I closed my eyes and held my breath.

It hurt bad. Real bad. But I managed, half-blind, to drag myself and Annie down the burning stairs. She was dead. I didn't know that at the time. Me, I came within a hair of dying. Stagecoach drove into town the day after and found me. Raced me to the hospital in Santa Fe.

And that's how Stinking Springs met its end.

"That's also how a young whelp of eighteen learned what pleases women and gained his blessed longevity by regularly practicing what Hefty Jake Gentry had preached on main street," said Kyle, his caring hands massaging his lovers' open secrets.

Tiffany's panties were sopping. She rose to remove them, unhooking and discarding her bra as she stood.

"Jake somehow straddled that whomp of flame. 'Twas almost as though his spirit rode straight into me. He gave me staying power, a pleasing technique (or so they tell me), and an abiding love for all womankind, for the mystery of them and for their magic. *Your* magic, my dear Tiffany. That's right. You don't need those panties anymore. They profane your sacred flesh."

20

Tiffany felt the yield of tufted carpet beneath her feet as she walked to Kyle, stood before him, reached both hands beneath her belly and kneaded herself. "Do you like the way I look, Kyle?" From the adoration in his eyes and the way his manhood strained at its seams in triple blush, she already knew the answer. But she wanted to hear him say it in that rich baritone of his.

"I love the way you look, dear heart. I love *you*, Miss Tiffany Walker. I love the fuck out of you. And if you don't spindle your lovely cunt on my ramrod of a cock this instant, you're going to make dear old Kyle Hardwick a very miserable old man indeed."

Tiffany spared him that fate.

CLAP IF YOU BELIEVE

I understand her parents' wariness. A woman like my Tinkerbell is bound to attract the amorous attentions of the wrong sort now and again. So when they open the door and appraise me like a suspect gem, not smiling, not yet inviting me in, I understand and forbear. "Good evening," I say, and let the silence float like untroubled webs of gossamer between us.

After a time, Mr. Jones turns to his wife and says, "What do you think?"

"The eyes look reasonably sane," she replies, to his nod, "though that's not always an airtight indicator these days and there is a worrisome edge to them."

I look down, stifling the urge to defend myself, and am gratified to hear Mr. Jones say, "Man with his hobbies and profession is bound to have sharp eyes. I say we give him the benefit and let him in."

She sighs. "Oh, all right. Come in out of the heat, young man. Put your shoes there." A serried rank of them faces the wall like naughty students: practical ones for Mr. and Mrs. Jones, scuffed high-tops for twelve-year-old Melissa, and, looking more like shed leaves than footwear, Tinkerbell's familiar green-felt slippers. I unknot and loosen my buffed black Florsheims and set them beside my beloved's footwear, thinking what a marvel her tiny feet are and how delightful it is—ensconced alone in her cozy apartment after a date—to take her legs, right up to the thighs, into my mouth and lightly tongue those feet, her tiny soles, the barely perceptible curve

22

of her insteps, the sheer white-corn delicacy of her ten tiny toes. How ecstatically my darling pixie writhes and wriggles in my hand, her silver-sheened wings fluttering against my palm!

"Hi, Alex." I look up and there's Melissa standing by an archway that leads to the dining room.

"Hi, Melissa," I say, wiggling my fingers at her like Oliver Hardy fiddling with his tie. The zoo is only four blocks from their house and we've begun, Melissa and Tink and I, to make a regular thing of meeting there Saturday afternoons. Once, over snow cones, Melissa told me that Tink had been miserable for a long time, "but now that you've come into her life, Alex," this from a twelve-year-old, "she flits about like a host of hummingbirds when she drops in for Sunday dinner and makes loads of happy words twinkle in my head, in all of our heads." Hearing Melissa say that made me glad, and I told her so.

Melissa giggles at my finger-waggling and says, "Come on in and sit down."

I look a question at the Joneses. Mrs. Jones gives an unreadably flat lip-line to me. Mr. Jones, instead of seconding Melissa's invitation, comes up like an old pal, leans in to me, and says, "You and me, after dinner, over cigars in my study."

I'm not sure what he's getting at, but I feel as if he's somehow taken me into his confidence. I say, "That's fine, sir," and that seems to satisfy him because he steps back like film reversed and stands beside his wife.

A familiar trill rises in my brain. The others turn their heads, as do I, to the stairs, its sweeping mahogany banister soaring into the warm glow upstairs. And down flies my beloved Tinkerbell, trailing behind her a silent burst of stars. Her lovely face hovers before me, the tip of her wand describing figure-eights in the air. "Hello, Alex my lovely," she hums into my head. Then she flits to my cheek, the perfect red bow of her lips burning cinnamon kisses there. Recalling the sear of those kisses on other parts of my anatomy, I feel a blush rising.

"Tinkerbell," I say, using her full name, "perhaps we should—"

"Yes, daughter," Mrs. Jones breaks in, clearly not at all amused, "your young man is correct. Dinner's on the table." She glares at me and turns to lead the party into the dining room. Melissa comes and takes my hand, while Tink flits happily about my right shoulder, singing into my head her gladness at seeing me. When she holds still long enough for me to fix a discerning eye on her, I'm relieved to see that she's not yet showing.

Once dinner is under way, the ice thins considerably and in fact Tink's mother rushes past her more cautious husband to become my closest ally. Maybe her change of heart is brought on by my praise for her rainbow trout amandine—which praise I genuinely mean. Or maybe it's brought on by the dinner conversation, which focuses on me half the time, on Tink the other half. Mrs. Jones asks surprisingly insightful questions about my practice as a microsurgeon, pleasantly coaxing me into more detail than the average non-medico cares to know about the handling of microsutures and the use of interchangeable oculars on a headborne surgical microscope. I'm happy to oblige as I watch Tinkerbell hover over her dinner, levitating bits of it with her wand—nothing flamboyant, merely functional— and bringing it home to her mouth.

After some perfunctory questions about my butterfly collection (I've sold it since meeting their daughter, as it disquiets her) and my basement full of miniature homes and the precisely detailed furniture that goes with them (I met Tinkerbell at a show for just such items), the talk turns to their daughter. It's a little embarrassing, what with Melissa beaming at me, and Tinkerbell singing into me her bemusement at her mother, and her father looking ever more resigned, and his wife going on and on about her tiny daughter, giving me a mom's-eye view of her life history as if Tinkerbell herself weren't sitting at the table with us. Mrs. Jones is in the midst of telling how easy it was to give birth to a pixie and how hard to live with the fact thereafter when I suddenly laugh, quickly disguising it as a choke—water went down the wrong way, no problem, really I'm all right. Tink has made me a lewd and lovely proposition, one which has brought to mind the heartaching image of her as last I enjoyed her, looking so vulnerable with her glade-green costume and her slim wand set aside, arching back on her spun-silver wings, her perfect breasts thrust up like twin peaks on a relief map, her ultra-fine fingers kneading the ruddy pucker of her vulva, awaiting the tickle and swirl of my ultra-fine horsehair brush, the hot monstrosity of my tonguetip, and the perfect twin-kiss of my cock-slit, as we began our careful coitus.

I give Tink a quick stare of admonition—a joke and not a joke. She beams, melts me, and goes back to her meal. The entire scene suddenly amuses me greatly, this whole silly ritual of meeting the parents, getting their approval for the inevitable, most of which—in particular the essential proof of the rightness of shared intimacy— has already come to pass. But I contain my laughter. I act the good son-in-law-to-be and show these kind narrow people, under whose love and tutelage my fiancée grew to maturity, the esteem and good manners they expect.

"Alex, would you please pass the peas?" says Melissa when her mother pauses to inhale. Mrs. Jones has launched into yet another diatribe against an educational system too unfeeling, too inflexible for special students like her Tinkerbell. Already under fire have come the lack of appropriate gymnastic equipment, the unfeeling cretinism of a certain driver-ed instructor, and Tinkerbell's unmet needs for special testing conditions in all her academic subjects. As I pass the peas, the head drama coach falls into the hopper of Mrs. Jones' tirade for refusing even to consider mounting a production of *Peter Pan* and giving Tink a chance to perform the character they've named her after, a casting inspiration Mrs. Jones is certain would have brought her daughter out of the cocoon of adolescent shyness years earlier than had been the case.

"But the worst of it, Alex," she says, and I thank God that she's spoken my name for the first time (and that it dropped so casually into the conversation), "is that no one in all those years has had the slightest clue how to teach Tink—or even how to discover—the uses of her wand, other than as an odd utensil and for occasional cleaning tricks. It might have kept this family solvent—"

"Emma," warns Mr. Jones, defensive.

"—well, more solvent than it was. It might have saved peoples' lives, cured disease, made world leaders see reason through their cages of insanity, brought all kinds of happiness flowing into peoples' hearts the world over." She asks me point blank to help her tiny daughter discover the full potential of her wand, and I promise I will. I don't mention of course that we've already found one amazing use for it in our lovemaking, a use that makes me feel incredibly good, incredibly potent, and incredibly loving toward Tinkerbell. It occurs to me at that moment, listening to Mrs. Jones' spirited harangue, that the wand might indeed have other uses and that perhaps one of them, a healing use, might reduce the failures and increase the triumphs I witness every day in the operating room. I get excited by this, nod more, stoke food into my mouth faster than is strictly polite. We're bonding, Mrs. Jones and I. She can feel it, I can feel it, Melissa is grinning like an idiot, and Tink is humming snatches of *Lohengrin* into my head. "I love you, Alex," she wind-chimes, "I love you and the horse you rode in on." Looking aside, I watch her playing with her food, wanding a slow reversed meander of mashed potatoes into her mouth, biting it off in ribbons of white mush. Her unshod feet are planted apart on the damask and her wings, thin curved planes of iridescence, lie still against her back.

After dinner, Mrs. Jones is ready to usher me into the parlor for more bonding. But her husband holds up his hand to cut her off, saying, "It's time, Emma." "Oh," she says. He's got some bit of gristle in his craw, some one thing that's holding back his approval of me.

"Ah, the study," I say. "The cigars."

"Just so," he says in a way that suggests man-talk, and pretty serious man-talk at that. I follow him out of the dining room. Mrs. Jones and Melissa have odd looks on their faces. Even Tink's hum is edged with anxiety.

The study is dark and small, green-tinged and woodsy. There's a rolltop desk, now closed, and the rich smell of rolled tobacco and old ledgers pervades the air. He fits a green eyeshade around his head, offers me one. I accept but feel foolish in it, as if I'm at Disney World wearing a Donald Duck hat, bright yellow bill as brim.

Mr. Jones sits in a rosewood swivel chair and motions me to a three-legged ebony piano stool in front of him. I have to look up a good six inches to meet his eyes. "You smoke cigars?" he asks.

"Not unless you count one White Owl in my teens."

He chuckles once, then drops it. With a soft clatter of wood slats, he scrolls up the rolltop and opens a huge box of cigars. He lifts out two of them, big long thick cylinders of brown leaf with the smell of sin about them and the crisp feel of currency in their wrappings. I take what he offers and follow his lead in preparing, lighting, and puffing on the damned thing. I'm careful to control my intake, not wanting to lose face in a fit of coughing. The cigar tastes peculiarly pleasant, sweet, not bitter, and the back of my head feels like it's ballooning.

"My wife," he begins, "likes you. I like you. And Tinkerbell likes you, but then she's liked every last one of her boyfriends, even the slime-sucking shitwads—can we speak man to man?—who used Tink for their own degenerate needs and then discarded her."

I don't want to hear this.

"Not that there've been lots of men before you. She may be a pixie, our daughter, but she's got the good sense of the Joneses even so. But you know, Alex my boy, you'd be surprised at the number of men in this world who look and act perfectly normal, men whose mild exteriors cover sick vistas of muck and sludge, men who make regular guys like you and me ashamed to be called men."

"I assure you, sir, that—"

"—and I'd believe those assurances, I really would, even though I've believed and been fooled in the past. My little girl, Tinkerbell Titania Jones, is special to me as she is; not some freak, not a thing of shame or suspicion, no, but a thing of grace and beauty."

"She is indeed, Mr. Jones."

27

He fixes me in his glare and exhales a puff of blue smoke. It hangs like a miasma about him, but he doesn't blink. His eyes might be lizard eyes. "I had doubts when she was born, of course. What father wouldn't? No man likes to be deceived by his wife, not even through the irresistible agency of a stray faerie or incubus, if such there be in this world. But there are mannerisms of mine I recognized quite early in my daughter, mannerisms I was sure were neither learned nor trumped up by some phantom lover bent on throwing a cuckolded husband off his trail."

He cranes his neck and stares, about fifteen degrees askew of my face. It's a look I recognize from my first meeting with Tink at the miniaturists' show in Sacramento the previous winter. I'd asked her to dinner and she went all quiet and contemplative, looking just this way, before finally venturing a twinkled Yes. I could tell she'd been stung before, and recently.

"She's mine," he says. "Some mutation if you want to be cold-bloodedly clinical about it, but all mine. And I love her dearly, as parents of special children often do."

He takes a long puff, exhales it, looks at me. "Now I'm going to ask you three questions, Alex. Only truthful answers are going to win my daughter's hand."

I feel odd about this turn in the conversation, and yet the setting, the cigar smoke, the close proximity of this beast in his lair, make it seem perfectly normal. I nod agreement and flick a squat cylinder of ash into the open glass hand, severed, of a four-fingered man.

"First," Mr. Jones says, not stumbling over any of the words, "have you had sex with my daughter?"

My head is pounding. I take a long pull on my cigar and slowly exhale the smoke. My hand, holding it, seems big and beefy, unworthy of my incisive mind. "She and I have . . . made love, yes. We love each other, you see, and it's only natural for—"

"No extenuation," says Mr. Jones. "Your answer is Yes. It's a good answer, it's the truth, and I have no quarrel with it. I would think you some sort of nitwit if you hadn't worked out some mutually agreeable arrangement between you. No, I

28

don't want to know how it's done. I shudder to think about it. When she drops in, she seems none the worse for wear. If she's happy, and you're happy with her—and with the limitations you no doubt face—then that will content her mother and me."

I think of course of vaginal sinkings, that nice feel of being gripped there by a grown woman. And I think back years to my first girlfriend Rhonda, to her mouth, to the love she was kind enough to focus down below from time to time though less frequently than I would have preferred.

"That leads, of course, to my second question," says Mr. Jones, putting one hand, the one without the cigar, to his temple. "Will you be faithful to Tinkerbell, neither casting the lures of temptation toward other women nor consenting to be lured by them?"

I pause. "That's a complex question."

"It is indeed," he says, with a rising inflection that asks it all over again.

"I don't think," I tell him, my hands folded, my eyes deeply sincere, "I will ever fail my beloved in this way. Yet knowing the weakness of myself and other men, the incessant clamor of the gonads that I daresay all males are prey to, I hesitate to say Yes unequivocally to your question. But Tinkerbell gives me great satisfaction, and, more importantly, I believe I do the same for her. Something about her ways in bed, if you will, seems to silence the voice of lust when I'm around other women. Besides which—and I don't mean this flippantly— I've grown, through loving Tinkerbell, to appreciate smaller women. In fact, on the whole, I've come to find so-called normal-sized women unbearably gross and disgusting."

Mr. Jones looks askance at me. "Alex, you're a most peculiar man. But then I think that's what my daughter's going to need, a peculiar man, and yet it's so damned hard to know which set of peculiarities are the right ones."

I'm not sure how to take his comment, but then I'm in no position to debate the issue. "Yes, sir," I say.

"Almost out of the woods," says Mr. Jones, grinning. "The third one is easy." He tosses it off like a spent match: "Do you love Tinkerbell?"

This question throws me. It seems simple enough, but that's the problem: It's too simple. Does he want a one-word response, or a dissertation? Is it a trick question of some sort? And is the time I'm taking in deliberating over it actually sinking my chances? What is love, after all? Everybody talks about it, sings about it, yammers on and on endlessly about it. But it's so vague a word, and so loaded. I think of French troubadour poets, of courtly love and its manufacture, of Broadway show tunes and wall-sized faces saying "I love you" on big screens, saying it like some ritual curse or as if it signaled some terrible loss of control akin to vomiting.

And I say, "Yes and no," feeling my way into the open wound of shared camaraderie, ready to provide reasons for my equivocation, a brief discourse which will show him the philosophical depths of my musings and yet come about, in the end, to a grand paean of adoration for his daughter.

But before I can begin, he rises from his chair and reaches for me, and the next thing I know, the furniture hurtles by as if in a silent wind and the doors fly open seemingly without the intervention of human hands and I'm out on the street in front of their home, trying to stop my head from spinning.

It's dark out there but muggy. I ache inside, ache for my loss. It's not fair, I think. She loves me and I love her and by God we belong together. I'll call her in the morning when she's back in the city, I'll send roses, I'll surprise her with a knock on her door. We'll elope. This isn't the Dark Ages, after all. Tinkerbell and I don't need her parents' permission to marry.

Doors slam in the house. Downstairs, upstairs. A high-pitched voice, Melissa's, shouts something childish and angry, is answered by falsely calm parental soothings. None of the words can I make out.

The first floor goes dark after a while, then bit by bit the second. From where I'm standing, it looks like a miniature house, one of my basement models. I raise both hands and find I can obliterate it completely.

There is one golden glow of light hovering behind a drawn tan shade upstairs. Her bedroom, the room she grew up in. I want to clap my hands, clap them in defiance of her parents—she'll know what that means, she'll surely understand. But the energy has drained from my arms and they hang useless at my sides.

Behind the shade, my lost love's light moves slowly back and forth, back and forth, growing dimmer, casting forth ever smaller circles of gold with each beat of my heart.

RIDI BOBO

At first little things niggled at Bobo's mind: the forced quality of Kiki's mimed chuckle when he went into his daily pratfall getting out of bed; the great care she began to take painting in the teardrop below her left eye; the way she idly fingered a pink puffball halfway down her shiny green suit. Then more blatant signals: the creases in her crimson frown, a sign, he knew, of real discontent; the bored arcs her floppy shoes described when she walked the ruff-necked piglets; a wistful shake of the head when he brought out their favorite set of shiny steel rings and invited her, with the artful pleas of his expressive white gloves, to juggle with him.

But Bobo knew it was time to seek professional help when he whipped out his rubber chicken and held it aloft in a stranglehold—its eyes X'd shut in fake death, its pitiful head lolled against the back of his glove—and all Kiki could offer was a soundless yawn, a fatigued cock of her conical nightcap, and the curve of her back, one lazy hand waving bye-bye before collapsing languidly beside her head on the pillow. No honker would be brought forth that evening from her deep hip pocket, though he could discern its outline there beneath the cloth, a coy maddening shape that almost made him hop from toe to toe on his own. But he stopped himself, stared forlornly at the flaccid fowl in his hand, and shoved it back inside his trousers.

He went to check on the twins, their little gloved hands hugging the blankets to their chins, their perfect snowflake-white faces vacant with sleep. People said they looked more like Kiki than him, with their lime-green hair and the markings around their eyes. Beautiful boys, Jojo and Juju. He kissed their warm round red noses and softly closed the door.

In the morning, Bobo, wearing a tangerine apron over his bright blue suit, watched Kiki drive off in their new rattletrap Weezo, thick puffs of exhaust exploding out its tailpipe. Back in the kitchen, he reached for the Buy-Me Pages. Nervously rubbing his pate with his left palm, he slalomed his right index finger down the Snooper listings. Lots of flashy razz-ma-tazz ads, lots of zingers to catch a poor clown's attention. He needed simple. He needed quick. Ah! His finger thocked the entry short and solid as a raindrop on a roof; he noted the address and slammed the book shut.

Bobo hesitated, his fingers on his apron bow. For a moment the energy drained from him and he saw his beloved Kiki as she'd been when he married her, honker out bold as brass, doing toe hops in tandem with him, the shuff-shuff-shuff of her shiny green pants legs, the ecstatic ripples that passed through his rubber chicken as he moved it in and out of her honker and she bulbed honks around it. He longed to mimic sobbing, but the inspiration drained from him. His shoulders rose and fell once only; his sweep of orange hair canted to one side like a smart hat.

Then he whipped the apron off in a tangerine flurry, checked that the boys were okay playing with the piglets in the backyard, and was out the front door, floppy shoes flapping toward downtown.

Momo the Dick had droopy eyes, baggy pants, a shuffle to his walk, and an office filled to brimming with towers of blank paper, precariously tilted—like gaunt placarded and stilted clowns come to dine—over his splintered desk. Momo wore a battered old derby and mock-sighed a lot, like a bloodhound waiting to die.

He'd been decades in the business and had the dust to prove it. As soon as Bobo walked in, the tramp-wise clown seated behind the desk glanced once at him, peeled off his derby, twirled it, and very slowly very deliberately moved a stiffened fist in and out of it. Then his hand opened—red nails, white fingers thrust out of burst gloves—as if to say, Am I right?

Bobo just hung his head. His clownish hands drooped like weights at the ends of his arms.

The detective set his hat back on, made sympathetic weepy movements—one hand fisted to his eye—and motioned Bobo over. An unoiled drawer squealed open, and out of it came a puff of moths and a bulging old scrapbook. As Momo turned its pages, Bobo saw lots of illicit toe hops, lots of swollen honkers, lots of rubber chickens poking where they had no business poking. There were a whole series of pictures for each case, starting with a photo of his mopey client, progressing to the flagrante delicto evidence, and ending, almost without exception, in one of two shots: a judge with a shock of pink hair and a huge gavel thrusting a paper reading DIVORCE toward the adulterated couple, the third party handcuffed to a Kop with a tall blue hat and a big silver star on his chest; or two corpses, their floppy shoes pointing up like warped surfboards, the triumphant spouse grinning like weak tea and holding up a big pistol with a BANG! flag out its barrel, and Momo, a hand on the spouse's shoulder, looking sad as always and not a little shocked at having closed another case with such finality.

When Bobo broke down and mock-wept, Momo pulled out one end of a checkered hanky and offered it. Bobo cried long and hard, pretending to dampen yard upon yard of the unending cloth. When he was done, Momo reached into his desk drawer, took out a sheet with the word CONTRACT at the top and two X'd lines for signatures, and dipped a goose-quill pen into a large bottle of ink. Bobo made no move to take it but the old detective just kept holding it out, the picture of patience, and drops of black ink fell to the desktop between them.

Momo tracked his client's wife to a seedy Three-Ring Motel off the beaten path. She hadn't been easy to tail. A sudden rain had come up and the pennies that pinged off his windshield had reduced visibility by half, which made the eager Weezo hard to keep up with. But Momo managed it. Finally, with a sharp right and a screech of tires, she turned into the motel parking lot. Momo slowed to a stop, eying her from behind the brim of his sly bowler. She parked, climbed up out of the tiny car like a soufflé rising, and rapped on the door of Room Five, halfway down from the office.

She jiggled as she waited. It didn't surprise Momo, who'd seen lots of wives jiggle in his time. This one had a pleasingly sexy jiggle to her, as if she were shaking a cocktail with her whole body. He imagined the bulb of her honker slowly expanding, its bell beginning to flare open in anticipation of her little tryst. Momo felt his bird stir in his pants, but a soothing pat or two to his pocket and a few deep sighs put it back to sleep. There was work afoot. No time nor need for the wild flights of his long-departed youth.

After a quick reconnoiter, Momo went back to the van for his equipment. The wooden tripod lay heavy across his shoulder and the black boxy camera swayed like the head of a willing widow as he walked. The rest—unexposed plates, flash powder, squeezebulb—Momo carried in a carpetbag in his free hand. His down-drawn mouth puffed silently from the exertion, and he cursed the manufacturers for refusing to scale down their product, it made it so hard on him in the inevitable chase.

They had the blinds down but the lights up full. It made sense. Illicit lovers liked to watch themselves act naughty, in Momo's experience, their misdoings fascinated them so. He was in luck. One wayward blind, about chest high, strayed leftward, leaving a rectangle big enough for his lens. Miming stealth, he set up the tripod, put in a plate, and sprinkled huge amounts of glittery black powder along his flashbar. He didn't need the flashbar, he knew that, and it caused all manner of problem for him, but he had his pride in the aesthetics of picture-taking, and he was willing to blow his cover for the sake of that pride. When the flash went off, you knew you'd taken a picture; a quick bulb squeeze in the dark was a cheat and not at all in keeping with his code of ethics.

So the flash flared, and the smoke billowed through the loud report it made, and the peppery sting whipped up into Momo's nostrils on the inhale. Then came the hurried slap of shoes on carpet and a big slatted eyelid opened in the blinds, out of which glared a raging clownface. Momo had time to register that this was one hefty punchinello, with muscle-bound eyes and lime-green hair that hung like a writhe of caterpillars about his face. And he saw the woman, Bobo's wife, honker out, looking like the naughty fornicator she was but with an overlay of uh-oh beginning to sheen her eyes.

The old adrenaline kicked in. The usually poky Momo hugged up his tripod and made a mad dash for the van, his carpetbag shoved under one arm, his free hand pushing the derby down on his head. It was touch and go for a while, but Momo had the escape down to a science, and the beefy clown he now clouded over with a blanket of exhaust—big lumbering palooka caught off-guard in the act of chicken stuffing—proved no match for the wily Momo.

Bobo took the envelope and motioned Momo to come in, but Momo declined with a hopeless shake of the head. He tipped his bowler and went his way, sorrow slumped like a mantle about his shoulders. With calm deliberation Bobo closed the door, thinking of Jojo and Juju fast asleep in their beds. Precious boys, flesh of his flesh, energetic pranksters, they deserved better than this.

He unzippered the envelope and pulled out the photo. Some clown suited in scarlet was engaged in hugger-mugger toe hops with Kiki. His rubber chicken, unsanctified by papa church, was stiff-necked as a rubber chicken can get and stuffed deep inside the bell of Kiki's honker. Bobo leaned back against the door, his shoes levering off the rug like slapsticks. He'd never seen Kiki's pink rubber bulb swell up so grandly. He'd never seen her hand close so tightly around it nor squeeze with such ardency. He'd never ever seen the happiness that danced so brightly in her eyes, turning her painted tear to a tear of joy.

He let the photo flutter to the floor. Blessedly it fell facedown. With his right hand he reached deep into his pocket and pulled out his rubber chicken, sad purple-yellow bird, a male's burden in this world. The sight of it brought back memories of their wedding. They'd had it performed by Father Beppo in the center ring of the Church of Saint Canio. It had been a beautiful day, balloons so thick the air felt close under the bigtop. Father Beppo had laid one hand on Bobo's rubber chicken, one on Kiki's honker, inserting hen into honker for the first time as he lifted his long-lashed eyes to the heavens, wrinkle lines appearing on his meringue-white forehead. He'd looked to Kiki, then to Bobo, for their solemn nods toward fidelity.

And now she'd broken that vow, thrown it to the wind, made a mockery of their marriage.

Bobo slid to the floor, put his hands to his face, and wept. Real wet tears this time, and that astonished him, though not enough—no, not nearly enough—to divert his thoughts from Kiki's treachery. His gloves grew soggy with weeping. When the flood subsided, he reached down and turned the photo over once more, scrutinizing the face of his wife's lover. And then the details came together—the ears, the mouth, the chin; oh God no, the hair and the eyes—and he knew Kiki and this bulbous-nosed bastard had been carrying on for a long time, a very long time indeed. Once more he inventoried the photo, frantic with the hope that his fears were playing magic tricks with the truth.

But the bald conclusion held.

At last, mulling things over, growing outwardly calm and composed, Bobo tumbled his eyes down the length of the flamingo-pink carpet, across the spun cotton-candy pattern of the kitchen floor, and up the cabinets to the Jojo-and-Juju-proofed top drawer.

Bobo sat at his wife's vanity, his face close to the mirror. Perfume atomizers jutted up like minarets, thin rubber tubing hanging down from them and ending in pretty pink squeezebulbs Bobo did his best to ignore.

He'd strangled the piglets first, squealing the life out of them, his large hands thrust beneath their ruffs. Patty Petunia had pistoned her trotters against his chest more vigorously and for a longer time than had Pepper, to Bobo's surprise, she'd always seemed so much the frailer of the two. When they lay still, he took up his carving knife and sliced open their bellies, fixed on retrieving the archaic instruments of comedy. Just as his tears had shocked him, so too did the deftness of his hands—guided by instinct he'd long supposed atrophied—as they removed the bladders, cleansed them in the water trough, tied them off, inflated them, secured each one to a long thin bendy dowel. He'd left Kiki's dead pets sprawled in the muck of their pen, flies growing ever more interested in them.

Sixty-watt lights puffed out around the perimeter of the mirror like yellow honker bulbs. Bobo opened Kiki's cosmetics box and took out three squat shallow cylinders of color. The paint seemed like miniature seas, choppy and wet, when he unscrewed and removed the lids.

He'd taken a tin of black paint into the boys' room—that and the carving knife. He sat beside Jojo in a sharp jag of moonlight, listening to the card-in-bike-spoke duet of their snores, watching their fat wide lips flutter like stuck bees. Bobo dolloped one white finger with darkness, leaning in to X a cross over Jojo's right eyelid. If only they'd stayed asleep. But they woke. And Bobo could not help seeing them in new light. They sat up in mock-stun, living outcroppings of Kiki's cruelty, and Bobo could not stop himself from finger-scooping thick gobs of paint and smearing their faces entirely in black. But even that was not enough for his distracted mind, which spiraled upward into bloody revenge, even though it meant carving his way through innocence. By the time he plunged the blade into the sapphire silk of his first victim's suit, jagging open downward a bloody furrow, he no longer knew which child he murdered. The other one led him a merry chase through the house, but Bobo scruffed him under the cellar stairs, his shoes windmilling helplessly as Bobo hoisted him up and sank the knife into him just below the second puffball. He'd tucked them snug beneath their covers, Kiki's brood; then he'd tied their rubber chickens together at the neck and nailed them smackdab in the center of the heartshaped headboard.

Bobo dipped a brush into the cobalt blue, outlined a tear under his left eye, filled it in. It wasn't perfect but it would do.

As horsehair taught paint how to cry, he surveyed in his mind's eye the lay of the living room. Everything was in readiness: the bucket of crimson confetti poised above the front door; the exploding cigar he would light and jam into the gape of her mouth; the tangerine apron he'd throw in her face, the same apron that hung loose now about his neck, its strings snipped off and spilling out of its big frilly kangaroo pouch; the Deluxe Husband-Tamer Slapstick he'd paddle her bottom with, as they did the traditional high-stepping divorce chase around the house; and the twin bladders to buffet her about the ears with, just to show her how serious things were with him. But he knew, nearly for a certainty, that none of these would stanch his blood lust, that it would grow with each antic act, not assuaged by any of them, not peaking until he plunged his hand into the elephant's-foot umbrella stand in the hallway and drew forth the carving knife hidden among the parasols—whose handles shot up like cocktail toothpicks out of a ripple of pink chiffon—drew it out and used it to plumb Kiki's unfathomable depths.

Another tear, a twin of the first, he painted under his right eye. He paused to survey his right cheekbone, planning where precisely to paint the third.

Bobo heard, at the front door, the rattle of Kiki's key in the lock.

Momo watched aghast.

He'd brushed off with a dove-white handkerchief his collapsible stool in the bushes, slumped hopelessly into it, given a mock-sigh, and found the bent slat he needed for a splendid view of the front hallway and much of the living room, given the odd neck swivel. On the off-chance that their spat might end in reconciliation, Momo'd also positioned a tall rickety stepladder beside Bobo's bedroom window. It was perilous to climb and a balancing act and a half not to fall off of, but a more leisurely glimpse of Kiki's lovely honker in action was, he decided, well worth the risk.

What he could see of the confrontation pleased him. These were clowns in their prime, and every swoop, every duck, every tumble, tuck, and turn, was carried out with consummate skill. For all the heartache Momo had to deal with, he liked his work. His clients quite often afforded him a front row seat at the grandest entertainments ever staged: spills, chills, and thrills, high passion and low comedy, inflated bozos pin-punctured and deflated ones puffed up with triumph. Momo took deep delight—though his forlorn face cracked nary a smile—in the confetti, the exploding cigar, what he could see and hear of their slapstick chase. Even the bladder-buffeting Bobo visited upon his wife strained upward at the down-droop of Momo's mouth, he took such fond joy in the old ways, wishing with deep soundless sighs that more clowns these days would re-embrace them.

His first thought when the carving knife flashed in Bobo's hand was that it was rubber, or retractable. But there was no drawn-out scene played, no mock-death here; the blow came swift, the blood could not be mistaken for ketchup or karo syrup, and Momo learned more about clown anatomy than he cared to know—the gizmos, the coils, the springs that kept them ticking; the organs, more piglike than clownlike, that bled and squirted; the obscure voids glimmering within, filled with giggle power and something deeper. And above it all, Bobo's plunging arm and Kiki's crimped eyes and open arch of a mouth, wide with pain and drawn down at the corners by the weight of her dying.

Momo drew back from the window, shaking his head. He vanned the stool, he vanned the ladder. There would be no honker action tonight. None, anyway, he cared to witness. He reached deep into the darkness of the van, losing his balance and bellyflopping so that his legs flew up in the night air and his white shanks were exposed from ankle to knee. Righting himself, he sniffed at the red carnation in his lapel, took the inevitable faceful of water, and shouldered the pushbroom he'd retrieved.

The neighborhood was quiet. Rooftops, curved in high hyperbolas, were silvered in moonlight. So too the paved road and the cobbled walkways that led up to the homes on Bobo's side of the street. As Momo made his way without hurry to the front door, his shadow eased back and forth, covering and uncovering the brightly lit house as if it were the dark wing of the Death Clown flapping casually, silently, overhead. He hoped Bobo would not yank open the door, knife still dripping, and fix him in the red swirl of his crazed eyes. Yet maybe that would be for the best. It occurred to Momo that a world which contained horrors like these might happily be left behind. Indeed, from one rare glimpse at rogue-clown behavior in his youth, as well as from gruesome tales mimed by other dicks, Momo thought it likely that Bobo, by now, had had the same idea and had brought his knife-blade home.

This case had turned dark indeed. He'd have lots of shrugging and moping, much groveling and kowtowing to do, before this was over. But that came, Momo knew, with the territory. Leaning his tired bones into the pushbroom, he swept a swatch of moonlight off the front stoop onto the grass. It was his duty, as a citizen and especially as a practitioner of the law, to call in the Kops. A few more sweeps and the stoop was moonless; the lawn to either side shone with shattered shards of light. He would finish the walkway, then broom away a spill of light from the road in front of Bobo's house, before firing the obligatory flare into the sky.

Time enough then to endure the noises that would tear open the night, the clamorous bell of the mismatch-wheeled pony-drawn firetruck, the screaming whistles in the bright red mouths of the Kops clinging to the Kop Kar as it raced into the neighborhood, hands to their domed blue hats, the bass drums booming as Bobo's friends and neighbors marched out of their houses, spouses and kids, poodles and ponies and piglets highstepping in perfect columns behind.

For now, it was enough to sweep moonlight from Bobo's cobbled walkway, to darken the wayward clown's doorway, to take in the scent of a fall evening and gaze up wistfully at the aching gaping moon.

LI'L MISS
ULTRASOUND

June 30, 2004
Mummy dearest,

It's great to hear from you, though I'm magnitudinously distraught that you can't be here for the contest. Still, I'm not complaining. It's extremely better that you show up for the birth—three weeks after my little munchkin's copped her crown!—and help out afterwards. The contest is a hoot and I want to do you proud, I *will* do you proud, but that can be done from a distance too, don't you think? What with the national coverage and the mega-sponsorship, you'll get to VCR me and the kid many times over. And of course I'll save all the local clippings for you like you asked.

It made my throat hurt, the baby even kicked, when you mentioned Willie in your last letter. It's tough to lose such a wonderful man. Still, he died calmly. I read that gruesome thing a few years ago, that *How We Die* book? It gave me the chills, Mom, how some people thrash and moan, how they don't make a pretty picture at all, many of them. Willie was one of the quiet ones though, thank the Lord. Nary a bark nor whimper out of him, he just drifted off like a thief in the night. Which was funny, because he was so, I don't know, *noisy* isn't the right word, I guess *expressive* maybe, his entire life.

Oh, before I close, I gotta tell you about Kip. Kip's my ultrasound man. I'm in love, I think. Kind face on him. Nice compact little bod. Cute butt too, the kind of buns you can

42

wrap your hands halfway around, no flabby sags to spoil your view or the feel of the thing. Anyway, Kip's been on the periphery of the contest for a few years and likes tinkering with the machinery. He's confided in me. Says he can—and will!—go beyond the superimposition of costumes that's been all the rage in recent years to some other stuff I haven't seen yet and he won't spell out. He worked some for those Light and Magic folks in California, and he claims he's somehow brought all that stuff into the ultrasound arena. Kip's sworn me to secrecy. He tells me we'll win easy. But I'm my momma's daughter. I don't put any stock in eggs that haven't been hatched, and Kip isn't fanatical about it, so it's okay. Also, Mother, he kissed me. Yep! As sweet and tasty as all get-out. I'll reveal more, next missive. Meantime, you can just keep guessing about what we're up to, since you refuse to grace us with your presence at the contest.

Just teasing, Mummy dear. Me and my fetal muffin will make you so proud, your chest will puff out like a Looney Tunes hen! Your staying put—for legit reasons, like you said—is a-okay with me, though I *do* wish you were here to hug, and chat up, and share the joy.

Love, love, love, mumsy mine,
Wendy

Kip brightened when Wendy came in from the waiting room, radiant with smiles.

Today was magic day. The next few sessions would acquaint Wendy with his enhancements to the ultrasound process. He wanted her confident, composed, and fully informed onstage.

"Wendy, hello. Come in." They traded hugs and he hung her jacket on a clothes rack.

"You can kiss me, you know," she teased.

He shook his head. "It doesn't feel right in the office. Well, okay, a little one. Mmmm. Wendy, hon, you're a keeper! Now hoist yourself up and let's put these pillows behind your back. That's the way. Comfy? Can you see the monitor?"

43

"Yes." Eagerly, she bunched her maternity dress up over her belly. Beautiful blue and red streaks, blood lightning, englobed it. A perfect seven-months' pooch. Her flowered briefs were as strained and displaced as a fat man's belt.

"Okay, now," said Kip. "Get ready for a surprise. This'll be cold." He smeared thick gel on her belly and moved the hand-held transducer to bring up baby's image. "There's our little darling."

"Mmmmm, I like that 'our'!"

"She's a beauty *without* any enhancement, isn't she? Now we add the dress." Reaching over, he flipped a switch on his enhancer. Costumes had come in three years before, thanks to the doctor Kip had studied under. They were now expected fare. "Here's the one I showed you last time," he said, pink taffeta with hints of chiffon at the bodice. There slept baby in her party dress, her tiny fists up to her chest.

"It's beautiful," enthused Wendy. "You can almost hear it rustle." What a joy Wendy was, thought Kip. A compact little woman who no doubt would slim down quickly after giving birth.

"Okay. Here goes. Get a load of this." He toggled the first switch. Overlaying the soft fabric, there now sparkled sequins, sharp gleams of red, silver, gold. They winked at random, cutting and captivating—spliced in, by digital magic, from a captured glisten of gems.

"Oh, Kip. It's breathtaking."

It was indeed. Kip laughed at himself for being so proud. But adding sparkle was child's play, and he fully expected other ultrasounders to have come up with it this year. It wouldn't win the contest. It would merely keep them in the running. He told Wendy so.

"Ah but this," he said, "this will put us over the top." He flipped the second switch, keeping his eyes not on the monitor but on his lover, knowing that the proof of his invention would be found in the wideness of her eyes.

Eudora glared at the monitor.

She had won the Li'l Miss Ultrasound contest two years

44

running—the purses her first two brats brought in had done plenty to offset the bother of raising them—and she was determined to make it three.

Then she could retire in triumph.

She had Moe Bannerman, the best ultrasound man money could buy. He gestured to the monitor's image. "She's a beaut. Do you have a name yet?"

"Can the chatter, Moe. I'll worry about that after she wins. Listen, I'm dying for a smoke. Let's cut to the chase."

Moe's face fell.

Big friggin' deal, she thought. Let him cry to his fat wife, then dry his tears on the megabucks Eudora was paying him.

"Here she is, ready for a night on the town." He flipped a switch and her kid was swaddled in a svelte evening gown, a black number with matching accessories (gloves and a clutch-purse) floating beside her in the amniotic sac.

Eudora was impressed. "Clear image."

"Sharpest yet. I pride myself on that. It's the latest in digital radiography, straight from Switzerland. We use intensity isocontours to—"

"It looks good. That's what counts. We win this round. Good. Now what about the swimsuit?"

"Ah. A nice touch. Take a look." Again his hands worked their magic. "See here. A red bikini with white polka dots."

"The sunglasses look ordinary, Moe. Give her better frames, a little glitz, something that catches the eye."

"I'll have some choices for you next time."

She shot a fingertip at him. "To hell with choices. You get the right ones first time, or I'll go to someone else." She'd heard rumor of a new ultrasound man on the horizon, Kip Johnson. He deserved a visit, just to check out the terrain. Handsome fuck, scuttlebutt said.

"Yes, ma'am. But take a look at this. It'll win us this round too. We show them the bikini, a nice tight fit that accentuates your baby girl's charms. I've even lent a hint of hardness to her nipples, which will most likely net you a contract with one of the baby-formula companies. But watch. We flip a switch and . . ."

45

Eudora had her eyes on the screen, her nicotine need making more vivid the image she saw. It was as if the kid had been suddenly splashed with a bucket of water. No twitch of course. It was all image. But the swimsuit's fabric lost its opacity. See-through. Gleams of moisture on her midriff. Her nipple nubs grew even harder, and her pudendal slit was clearly outlined and highlighted. Moe, you're a genius, she thought.

"Cute," she said. "What else you got?"

Thus she strung the poor dolt along, though his work delighted her. Dissatisfaction, she found, tended to spur people to their best. It wouldn't do to have Moe resting on his laurels. People got trounced by surprise that way. Eudora was determined not to be one of them.

When they were done, she left in a hurry, had a quick smoke, and hit the road. The Judge was due for a visit. There were other judges, of course, all of whom she did her best to cultivate. But somehow Benjamin—perversely he preferred the ugly cognomen "Benj"—was The Judge, a man born to the role.

Weaving through traffic, she imagined the slither of his hand across her belly.

Benj walks into the house without knocking.

In the kitchen he finds her dull hubby, feeding last year's winner (Gully or Tully) from a bottle. The beauty queen from two years prior toddles snot-nosed after him, wailing, no longer the tantalizing piece of tissue she had once been. Her name escapes him.

But names aren't important. What's important are *in utero* images and the feelings they arouse in him.

"Hello, Chet," says Benj.

Stupid Chet lights up like a bulb about to burn out. "Oh, hi, Benj. Eudora's in the bedroom. Have at her!"

Benj winks. "I will."

He winds his way through the house, noting how many knick-knacks prize money and commercial endorsements can buy. Over-the-hill, post-fetal baby drool is all *he* sees on the tube once the little darlings are born. It never makes him want to buy a thing.

"Why, Benjamin. Hello." She says it in that fake provocative voice, liking him for his power alone of course. As long as he can feel her belly, he doesn't care.

"Touch it?" he asks in a boyish voice. "Touch it now?" He thickens below.

"Of course you can," says Eudora, easing the bedroom door shut and leaning against it, her hands on the knob as if her wrists are tied.

Stupid Chet thinks Benj and Eudora do the man-woman thing. Chet wants money from the winnings, so he's okay with it as long as they use rubbers. But they don't *really* do the man-woman thing. Nope. They just tell Chet they do. Benj rubs her belly and feels the object of his lust kick and squirm in there, touching herself, no doubt, with those tiny curled hands, thrashing around breathless in the womb, divinely distracted.

Breathless.

Baby's first breath taints absolutely.

"Touch yourself, Benjamin."

He does. He wears a rubber, rolled on before he left the car. Later, he'll give it to Eudora so she can smear it with her scent and drop it in the bathroom wastebasket. Chet's a rummager, a sniffer. It's safer to provide him evidence of normalcy.

To Benj, normal folks are abnormal. But it takes all kinds to make a world.

His mouth fills with saliva. Usually, he remembers to swallow. Sometimes, a teensy bit drools out.

The baby kicks. Benj's heart leaps up like a frisky lamb. Eudora pretends to get off on this, but Benj knows better. He ignores her, focusing on his arousal, and is consumed with bliss.

July 12, 2004
Mummy dearest,

I'm so excited! Kip is too! The contest cometh tomorrow, so you'll see this letter *after* you've watched me and the munchkin on TV, but what the hey.

I could do without the media hoopla of course, though I suppose it comes with the territory. The contest assigns you these big bruisers, kind of like linebackers. I don't think you had them in your day. They deflect press hounds for you, so you don't go all exhausted from the barrage or get put on the spot by some persistent sensationalist out to sell dirt.

Then there are the protesters.

Ugh! I agree with you, mumsy. They're out of their blessed noggins. Both sorts of protesters. There are the ones who want the contest opened up to second trimester fetuses. The extremists even scream for first trimester. What, I ask you, would be the point of *that*?

Then there are the ones who want to ban pre-birth beauty contests entirely. Life-haters I call them. Hey, I'm as deep as the next gal. But I was never harmed by having a beauty queen for a mother nor by winning the Baby Miss contest when I was three months old. All that helped me, I'm sure—my self-esteem, my comfort with putting my wares on display, which a gal has just got to do to please her fella. I don't mind if Kip likes me for *all* of me, and I sincerely and honestly believe he does. But that includes the packaging. The sashay too, though mine's got *waddle* written all over it these days. Hey, I can work off the belly flab as soon as my baby's born. I know I can. I'll slim down and tighten up you-know-where even if it's under the knife with sutures taking up the slack. That's a woman's duty, as my momma taught me so well!

My point is that I'm *all* of me, the brainy stuff and the sexy stuff too. It's all completely me, it's my soul, and right proud of it am I. Well, listen to me gas on and on, like a regular old innerlectual. What hath thou raised? Or more properlike, whom?

Wish us luck, mumsikins!

Your loving and devoted daughter,
Wendy

***

Kip was alone in his office, making final tweaks to his software. Wendy had been by, an hour before, for one last run-through prior to their appearance onstage.

Five more minutes and he would lock up.

His ultrasound workstation, with its twenty-four-inch, ultra-high-resolution, sixteen-million-color monitor, had become standard for MRI and angiography. Moe Bannerman, last year's winning ultrasound man, had copped the prize, thanks to this model. But Kip was sure, given the current plateau in technology, that whatever Moe had up his sleeve this year would involve something other than the size and clarity of the image.

Butterflies flitted in Kip's gut. Somehow, no matter how old you got, exposure to the public limelight jazzed you up.

The outer office door groaned. Maisie coming back for forgotten car keys, thought Kip.

A pregnant woman appeared at the door. Eyes like nail points. Hair as long and shiny as a raven's wing. Where had he seen her? Ah. Moe's client, mother of the last two contest winners.

Wendy's competition.

"Hello there," she said, her voice as full-bellied as she was. "Have you got a minute?" She waddled in without waiting for an answer. "I'm Eudora Kelly."

He opened his mouth to introduce himself.

"You're Kip, if I'm not mistaken. My man will be going up against you tomorrow."

"True. Look, according to the rules, you and I shouldn't be talking."

She approached him. "Rules are made to keep sneaky people in line. We're both above board. At least, I am." Her voice was edged with tease, a quality that turned Kip off, despite the woman's stunning looks. "Besides, even if I were to tell Moe what you and I talked about or what we did—which I won't—it's too late for him to counter it onstage, don't you think?"

"Ms. Kelly, maybe you'd better—"

She touched his arm, her eyes intent on the contours of his shirtsleeve. "I'll tell you what surprises *he's* planning to pull tomorrow. How would that be?"

"No, I don't want to know that." He did, of course, but such knowledge was off limits. She knew that as well as he.

"They say you've got new technologies you're drawing on. A background in the movies. Maybe next year, you and I could pair up."

Kip reviewed his helpers, looking for a blabbermouth.

No one came to mind.

"In fact," she sidled closer, her taut belly pressing against his side, "maybe *right now* we could pair up." Her hand touched his chest and drifted lower.

"All right, that's enough. There's the door. Use it." His firmness surprised him. It was rare to encounter audacity, rarer still therefore to predict how one would respond to it. He took her shoulders and turned her about, giving her a light shove.

She wheeled on him. "You think you're God, you spin some dials and flick a few switches. Well, me and Moe're gonna wipe the floor with your ass tomorrow. Count on it!"

Then she was gone.

The back of Kip's neck was hot and tense. "Jesus," he said, half expecting her to charge in for another try.

Giving the workstation a pat, he prepared to leave, making sure that the locks were in place, the alarms set.

"Fool jackass," Eudora said. "The man must be sexed the wrong way around."

"Some people," observed the judge, his eyes on her beach ball belly, "have a warped sense of right and wrong. They take that Sunday school stuff for gospel, as I once did long ago."

"Not me, Benjamin. I knew it for the crock it was the moment it burbled out of old Mrs. Pilsner's twisted little mouth. Ummm, that feels divine." It didn't, but what the hell. Benjamin would be pivotal tomorrow. No sense letting the truth spoil her chances.

The judge's moist hand moved upon her, shaky with

what was happening elsewhere. Soon he would yank out his tool, a condom the color of rancid custard rolled over it like a liverwurst sheath. "Yeah, I wised up when I saw how the wicked prospered," he said. "How do you *do* it, Eudora? This is the third sexy babe in a row. Your yummy little siren is calling to me."

"She wants it, Benjamin," said Eudora.

Perv city, she thought. It would be a relief to jettison this creep as soon as the crown was hers. Three wins. She would retire in glory and wealth. At the first sign he wanted to visit, she would drop him cold. No bridges left to burn after her triumph. Let the poor bastard drool on someone else's belly.

Benjamin groped about between the parted teeth of his zipper. Eudora said, "That Kip person's going to spring something."

"Who's he?" asked the judge, pulling out his plum.

"You know. The ultrasound guy that Wendy bubblehead is using. Scuttlebutt says he's doing something fancy."

"Ungh," said Benjamin.

Eudora pictured Kip's office receptionist, her hand shaking as she took Eudora's money. She was disgustingly vague and unhelpful, Maisie of the frazzled hair and the troubled conscience. All she gave off were echoes of unease: he has this machine, I don't know what it does, but it's good because he says it is and because they both look so sure of themselves after her visits. Worthless!

"My baby girl's getting off, hon."

"Me too," he gasped.

"You're a sweet man," she said. "Show us your stuff. Give it to us, Benjamin, right where we live. That's it. That's my sweet Benjamin Bunny."

Benj really gets into it. Eudora's bellyskin is so smooth and tight, and as hot as a brick oven. He smells baby oil in his memory.

Eudora has no cause for worry, he thinks. Moe Bannerman's a stellar technician. What Moe's able to do to tease naked babes into vivid life onscreen is nothing short of miraculous.

51

Benj conjures up the looker inside Eudora's womb by recalling what hangs on his bedroom wall, those stunning images from *Life* last year—better than the real thing though a boner's a boner no matter how you slice it.

He dips into Tupperwared coconut oil, smearing it slick and liberal upon her belly, as he does upon his condomed boytoy. Oil plays havoc with latex, he knows, but Benj isn't about to get near impregnation or STDs.

Benj bets Moe Bannerman will carry his experiments in vividness forward in the coming years. Headphones will caress Benj's head as he judges, the soft gurgle of fetal float-and-twist tantalizing his ears, vague murmurs coaxed by a digital audio sampler into a whispered *fuck-me* or *oh-yeah-baby*.

Or perhaps virtual reality will come of age. He'll put on goggles and gloves, or an over-the-head mask that gooses his senses into believing he's tasting her, the salty tang of preemie quim upon his tongue, the touch of his fingertips all over her white-corn-kernel body.

Benj shuts his eyes.

Eudora starts to speak but Benj says, "Hush," and she does. This time the rhythms are elusive but *there*, within reach if his mind twists the right way. The beauty queen to be is touching him, indeed she is, those tiny strong little fingers wrapped about his pinkie. Her eyelids are closed, the all-knowing face of the not-yet-born, lighting upon uncorrupted thoughts, unaware of and unbothered by the sensual filtering imposed by society on the living.

Her touch is as light as a hush of croissant crust. This, he thinks, is love: the wing-brush of a butterfly upon an eyelash; a sound so faint it throws hearing into doubt; a vision so fleetingly imprinted on the retina, it might be the stray flash of a neuron.

With such slight movements, love coaxes him along the path, capturing, keeping, and cultivating—like a seasoned temptress—the focus of his fascination, so that the path swiftly devolves into a grade, hurrying him downhill and abruptly thrusting him into a chute of pleasure. He whips and rumbles joyously along its oily sides once more, *once more, ONCE MORE!*

July 13, 2004
Mummy mine,

I'm writing from the convention center, just having come offstage from Round One, where our little dolly garnered her first *first*! I had a hunch I'd want to disgorge all these glorious pent-up emotions into my momma's ear. So I brought along my lilac stationery and that purple pen with the ice-blue feather you love so much. Here I sit in the dressing room with the nine other contestants who survived Round One. Ooh, the daggers that are zipping across the room from Eudora Kelly, whose kids won the last two years. Methinks she suspects we've got her skunked!

Baby's jazzed, doing more than her usual poking and prodding. Kip just gave me a peck (would it had been a bushel!!!) and left to check out his equipment for Round Two. If I were a teensy bit naughtier, I'd mention how much *fun* it is to check out Kip's equipment, ha ha ha. But you raised a daughter with that rarest of qualities, modesty. Besides which, it would be unseemly to get too much into that, Willie being so recently deceased and all. But life goes on. Oh boy howdy, does it ever!

I passed through those idiotic protesters with a minimum of upset, thanks to my linebacker types. Joe, he's the beefiest, flirts outrageously, but both of us know it's all in fun. Still, he's a sweetie and you should see the scowl that drops down over his face whenever some "news twerp" (that's what Joe calls them) sticks his neck out where it don't belong, begging Joe to lop it off.

There were twenty of us to start with. 'Taint so crowded here no more! The audience sounds like an ocean, and the orchestra—you heard me, strings and all, scads of them, like Mantovani—set all things bobbing on a sea of joy. Kip gave me a big kiss right here where I sit—no, you slyboots, on my lips!!! Before I knew it, I was standing onstage amidst twenty bobbing bellies, all of us watching our handsome aged wreck of a TV host, that Guy Givens you like so much, his bowtie jiggling up and down as he spoke, and his hand mike held just so. The judges were in view, including the drooly one—you

53

know, the one whose hanky is always all soppy by the end.

First off, oh joy, we got to step up and do those cutesy interviews. Who the heck can remember what I gassed on about? I guess they build suspense at least in the hall. At home, all I remember is that you and me and Dad used that dumb chit-chat as an excuse to grab a sandwich or a soda.

Then Round One was upon us, and we were number 16, not a great number but not all that bad neither. I lifted my dress for Kip—not the *first* time I've done that, I assure you!!!—to bare my belly and of course to show off my dazzling red-sequined panties. For good luck, I sewed, among the new sequins, an even dozen from my Baby Miss swimsuit. The crowd loved my dumpling's first outfit, a ball gown that might have waltzed in from the court of Queen Victoria. It reminded me of a wedding cake, what with all the flounces and frills and those little silver sugar bee-bees you and I love so much. Baby showed it off beautifully, don't you think?

Then Kip played his first card. With a casual gesture, he brought life to her face. Of course, her face *has* life, but it's a pretty placid sort of life at this stage, what with every need being satisfied as soon as it happens. So there's nothing to cry about and no air to cry with if she *could* cry.

Then it blossomed on her face: a flush and blush of tasteful makeup spreading over her cheeks and chin and forehead, a smear of carmine on her lips, turquoise blue eyeshadow and an elongation of her lashes. Huge monitors in the hall gave everyone as clear a picture as the folks at home on their TVs. I could taste the rush of amazement rippling through the hall at each effect.

Then, her darling eyes opened! Just for a second before Kip erased the image. Of course they didn't *really* open, any more than my baby really wore a ball gown. But they weren't just some painted porcelain doll's eyes. Kip's years in Hollywood paid off, because you would have sworn there was angelic intelligence in the deep gaze Kip gave her face—

Oops, we just got the five-minute call, mumsy, so I'll cut off here and pick back up at the next break. Wish us luck! Gotta go!!!

***

Kip followed close behind a stagehand, who wheeled the ultrasound equipment to the tape marks, locked down the rollers, and plugged the cord into an outlet on the stage floor. Wendy had already settled into the stylish recliner. "Hello, darling," said Kip, taking her hand. Wendy returned his kiss. "How are you two?"

"Fine." Her voice wavered, but Kip judged it near enough to the truth.

The stage manager, clipboard at the ready, breezed by. "Two minutes," he said. Hints of garlic.

Beyond the curtain's muffle, the emcee pumped things up. A drum roll and a cymbal crash rushed the orchestra into an arpeggio swirling up to suggest magic and pixie dust. Kip squeezed Wendy's hand.

When the curtain rose, Guy Givens strode over. "And here's our first round winner, Miss Wendy Sales. Round she certainly is. And ready for another round, I hope. Wendy, how does it feel to be the winner of our evening wear competition?"

"Well, Guy," said Wendy, as he poked the mike at her mouth, "it feels great, but I don't bet on any horse until the race is over's what my momma taught me. All these great gals I've met? Their babies too? They're *all* winners as far as I'm concerned."

"Ladies and gentleman, let's give the little lady's generosity a big hand." The emcee's mike jammed up into his armpit so he could show the audience how to clap with gusto. Then it jumped back into his grip. "Wendy, with that attitude, you'll be a great mom indeed."

"I sincerely hope so."

Ignoring her answer: "And now . . . let's see your adorable little girl *in her bobbysoxer outfit!*" The tuxedoed man backed out of the spotlight, his free hand raised in a flourish.

Deftly fingering a series of switches, Kip hid his amusement at the emcee's tinsel voice, as the orchestra played hush-hush music and Wendy's child came into view.

A tiny pair of saddle shoes graced the baby's feet. Her poodle skirt (its usually trim stitched poodle gravid with a bellyful of pups) gave a slight sway. She wore a collared blouse of kelly green. A matching ribbon set off her tresses, which Kip had thickened and sheened by means of Gaussian and Shadow filters combined with histogram equalization.

When the crowd's applause began to fall off, Kip put highlights back into baby's face, an effect which brought the clapping to new heights.

As if in answer, Kip turned to two dials and began to manipulate them. The baby's eyes widened. She gave a coy turn of the head. Then her eyelids lowered and Kip wiped the image away.

The effect looked easy, but the work that had gone into making it happen was staggering. To judge by the shouts and cheers that washed over the stage, the crowd sensed that. Wendy glowed.

"*Judges?*" screamed Guy Givens into his mike.

One by one, down the row of five, 10s shot into the air. A 9 from a squint-eyed woman who never gave 10s drew the briefest of boos.

Wendy mouthed "I love you" at Kip, and he mouthed it back, as the music swirled up and the curtain mercifully shut out an ear-splitting din of delight.

Eudora watched from the wings as the TV jerkoff with the capped teeth and the crow's feet chatted up her only competition one last time.

The swimsuit round.

Moe's water-splash effect had gained Eudora an exceptional score, but from the look on the ultrasound man's face out there, that insufferable Kip Johnson, she was afraid he was poised to take the Wendy bitch and her unborn brat over the top.

Dump Moe.

Yep, Moe was a goner. Yesterday's meat. Spawn the loser inside her, let her snivel through life, whining for the tit withheld. A dilation and extraction might better suit. Tone up. Four months from now, let Chet poke her a few times. Stick one last bun in the oven.

Then, adrip with apologies, she would pay Kip another visit, playing to his goody-two-shoes side if that got him off. Hell, she'd even befriend his lover. If Wendy had a two-bagger in mind, Eudora would persuade her—strictly as a friend with her best interests at heart—to retire undefeated.

Onstage, that damned tantalizing womb image sprang to life again, this time dressed for the beach. Her swimsuit was a stylish fire-engine-red one-piece that drew the eye to her bosom, as it slashed across the thighs and arrowed into her crotch. Nice, but no great shakes.

Then the kid's face animated again. Eudora knew that this face would bring in millions. For months, it would be splashed across front pages and magazine covers. Then it would sell products like nobody's business.

Would it ever!

Instead of repeating its coy twist of the head, the intrauterine babe fluttered her eyelashes at the audience and winked. Then she puckered her lips and relaxed them. No hand came up to blow that kiss, but Eudora suspected that Kip would make that happen next year.

Her kid would be the one to blow a kiss. *Her* kid would idly brush her fingers past breast and thigh, while tossing flirtatious looks at Benjamin and viewers at home.

Eudora scanned the judges through a deafening wall of elation. There sat the oily little pervert, more radiant than she had ever seen him. Another year would pass, a year of wound-licking capped by her triumph, and Kip's, right here on this stage. *Then* she'd dump the drooler. One more year of slobber, she assured herself, would be bearable.

Eye on the prize, she thought. Keep your eye on the prize.

Benj is in heaven. His drenched handkerchief lies wadded in his right pants pocket. Fortunately, his left contained a forgotten extra, stuck together only slightly with the crust of past noseblows. It dampens and softens now with his voluminous drool.

The curtain sweeps open. Midstage stand the three victors, awaiting their reward.

57

Wendy's infant has quite eclipsed Eudora's in his mind. The third-place fetus? It scarcely raises a blip. Its mother comes forward to accept a small faux-sapphire tiara, a modest bouquet of mums, and a token check for a piddling sum. An anorexic blonde hurries her off.

Eudora's up next.

Replay pix of her bambina flash across a huge monitor overhead. Beneath her smile, she's steaming. He's in the doghouse for his votes; he knows that. But there's always next year. She needs him. She'll get over it.

A silver crown, an armful of daffodils, a substantial cash settlement, and off Eudora waddles into oblivion, her loser-kid's image erased from the monitor.

Then his glands ooze anew as the house erupts. Like a bazillion cap guns, hands clap as Wendy's pride and joy lights up the screen with that killer smile, that wink, oh god those lips.

"*AND HERE'S OUR QUEEN INDEED!*" screams Guy Givens, welcoming Wendy into his arms. Gaggles of bimbos stagger beneath armloads of roses. The main bimbo's burden is lighter, a gold crown bepillowed. Wendy puts a hand to her mouth. Her eyes well.

Then it happens.

Something shifts in the winner's face. She whispers to Givens, who relays whatever she has said to the crown-bearing blonde. Unsure what to do, the blonde beckons offstage, mouthing something, then walks away. Wendy leans against the emcee, who says "Hold on now" into his mike. A puddle forms on the stage where she is standing. "Is there a . . . do we have a . . . of course we do, yes, here he comes, folks."

Benj feels light-headed.

The rest drifts by like a river ripe with sewage. Spontaneous TV, the young doctor, the ultrasound man, a wheeled-in recliner, people with basins of water, with instruments, backup medical personnel. Smells assault him. Sights. Guy Givens gives a hushed blow-by-blow. And then, a wailing *thing* lifts out of the ruins of its mother, its head like a smashed fist covered in blood, wailing, wailing, endlessly wailing. Blanket wrap. The emcee raises his voice in triumph, lowering the tiny

58

gold crown onto the bloody bawler's brow.

It's a travesty. Benj is glad to be sitting down. He rests his head on his palms and cries, mourning the passing of the enwombed beauty who winked and nodded in his direction not five minutes before.

Is there no justice in the world, he wonders. Must all things beautiful end in squalor and filth?

He craves his condo. How blissful it will be to be alone there, standing beneath the punishing blast of a hot shower, then cocooning himself under blankets and nestling into the oblivion of sleep.

July 14, 2004
Mumsicle mine, now GRAN-mumsicle!

Well I guess that'll teach me to finish my letters when I can. I'll just add a little more to the one I never got 'round to wrapping up, and send you the whole kitten-kaboodle [sic, in case you think I don't know!], along with the newsclips I promised.

I'm sitting here in a hospital bed surrounded by flowers. Baby girl No-Name-Yet is dozing beside me, her rosebud lips moving in the air and making me leak like crazy. I do so love mommyhood!

But I never expected to give birth in public. They were all so nice to me at the contest, even that Eudora woman, who seems to have had a change of heart. That creepy drooly judge came up to wish me his best, but Kip rough-armed him away and said something to him before kicking him offstage. I'll have to ask Kip what that was all about.

Oh and Kip proposed! I knew he would, but it's always a thrill when the moment arrives, isn't it? I cried and cried with joy and Kip got all teary too. He'll make a great father, and I'm betting we spawn a few more winners before we're through. We'll give you plenty of warning as to when the wedding will be.

He's deflected the media nuts so far, until my strength is back. They're all so antsy to get at me. But meanwhile Kip's the hero of the hour. There's even talk of a movie of the week, with guess-who doing the special effects of course. But Kip tells me these movie deals usually aren't worth the hot air they're written on, so he and I shrug it off and simply bask bask bask!

I'll sign off now and get some rest, but I wanted to close by thanking you for being such a super mom and role model for me, growing up. You showed me I could really make something of myself in this world if I just persisted and worked my buns off for what I wanted.

I have.

It's paid off.

And I have you to thank for it. I love you, Mom. You're the greatest. Come down as soon as you can and say hello and kootchie-koo-my-little-snookums to the newest addition to the family. You'll adore her. You'll adore Kip too. But hey, hands off, girl, he's mine all mine!!!

Your devoted daughter,
Wendy

BUCKY GOES TO CHURCH

His real name was Vernon Stevens but folks called him Bucky on account of his teeth and his beaverish waddle and well, just because it was such a cute name and he was such a cute little fat boy, nothing but cuddles in infancy, an impish ball of pudge in childhood, primed to take on the role of blubbery punching bag in adolescence.

Kids caught on quick, called him names, taunted him, treated him about even with dirt. Bucky smiled back big and broad and stupid, as if he fed on abuse. The worst of them he tagged after, huffing and puffing, arms swinging wildly like gawky chicken wings, fat little legs jubbing and juddering beneath the overhang of his butt to keep up with them. "Wait up you guys," he'd whinny, "no fair, hey wait for me!" They'd jeer and call him Blubberbutt and Porky Orca and Barf Brain, and Bucky just seemed to lap up their torment like it was manna from heaven.

But, hey wuncha know it gang, somewheres in Bucky's head he was storing away all that hurt: the whippings at home from his old man's genuine cow-leather belt, a storm of verbal abuse stinging his ears worse than the smack of leather on his naked ass; the glares and snippery from his frowzy mama, she of the pinched stare, the worn, tattered faceflesh, the tipple snuck down her throat at every odd moment; the bark of currish neighbors yowling after him to keep his sneaks off their precious lawns; teachers turning tight smiles on him to show they didn't mind his obtuse ways, Bucky'd get by okay if he did his best, but they'd be triple goddamned if they were going to go out of their way to help him; and the kids, not one of them daring to be his friend (Arnie Rexroth got yanked out of first grade and shuffled off to Phoenix so he didn't count), all of them coming around quick enough to consensus, getting off on taking the fatboy's head for a spin on the carousel of cruelty, good for a laugh, a good way to get on with the guys, a great way to forget your problems by dumping them in the usual place—on Bucky Stevens's fat sweaty crewcut of a head.

Well one day, about the time Bucky turned fifteen, he woke to the mutterings of a diamond-edged voice inside his left frontal lobe. "Kill, Bucky, kill!" it told him, and, argue with it as he might, the voice at last grew stronger and more persuasive, until there was nothing to do but act on its urgings. So Bucky gathered all that hurt he'd been storing away and pedaled off to church one Sunday morning on his three-speed with his dad's big backpack tugging at his shoulders like a pair of dead man's hands. The weight of the hardware inside punched at his spine as he pedaled, though it was lighter by the bullets lodged in the bodies of his parents, who lay now, at peace and in each other's arms, propped up against the hot-water heater in the basement. He couldn't recall seeing such contentment on their faces, such a "bastard!"-less, "bitch!"-free silence settling over the house.

He pumped, did Bucky, pumped like a sweathog, endured the TEC-9 digging at his backbone, kept the churchful of tormentors propped up behind his forehead like a prayer. His fat head gidded and spun with the bloodrush of killing his folks: his dad, dense as a Neanderthal, the ex-marine in him trying to threaten Bucky out of it, arms flailing backward as his forehead swirled open like a poinsettia in sudden bloom, his beefy body slamming like a sledge into the dryer, spilling what looked like borscht vomit all over its white enamel top; his mom down on her knees in uncharacteristic whimper, then, realizing she was done for, snarling her usual shit at him until he told her to shut her ugly trap and jabbed the barrel into her left breast and, with one sharp squeeze of his finger, buckled her up like a midget actress taking a bloody bow, pouring out her heart for an audience of one.

Bucky crested the half-mile hill at Main and Summit. The steeple thrust up into the impossible cerulean of the sky like a virgin boy's New-England-white erection humping the heavens. Bucky braked, easing by Washington, Madison, Jefferson. The First Methodist Church loomed up like a perfect dream as he neared it. It was a lovely white box resting on a close-clipped lawn, a simple beautiful spired construction that hid all sorts of ugliness inside.

Coasting onto the sidewalk, Bucky wide-arced into the parking lot and propped his bike against a sapling. Off came the backpack, clanking to the ground. A car cruised by, a police car. Bucky waved at the cops inside, saw the driver unsmiling return a fake wave, false town cohesion, poor sap paid to suspect everyone, even some pudgy little scamp parking his bike in the church lot, tugging at the straps of a big bulky backpack. Grim flatfaced flatfoot, hair all black and shiny—stranded separately like the teeth at the thick end of an Ace comb—was going to wish he'd been one or two seconds later cruising Main Street, was going to wish like hell he'd seen the TEC-9 shrug out of its canvas confinement and come to cradle in Bucky's arms, yes indeed.

Not wanting to spoil the surprise, Bucky pulled his Ninja t-shirt out of the front of his jeans, pressed the cool metal of the weapon against his sweaty belly, and redraped his shirt over it.

He could hear muffled organ music as he climbed the wide white steps. The front doors, crowding about like blind giants, were off-white and tall. And good God if the music mumbling behind them wasn't Onward, Christian Soldiers, as wheezed and worried by a bloodless band of bedraggled grunts too far gone on the shellshock and homesickness of everyday life to get it up for the Lord.

Bucky tried the handle. The door resisted at first, then yielded outward.

The narthex was empty. Through the simulated pearls of Sarah Janeway's burbling organ music, Bucky could see an elaborate fan of church bulletins on the polished table stretched between the inner doors. Programs, the little kids called them. Through the window in the right inner door to the sanctuary, the back of a deacon's bald head hung like some fringed moon. Coach Hezel, that's who it was; Bucky's coach the year before in ninth grade, all those extra laps for no good reason, pushups without end, and the constant yammer of humiliation: how Bucky had no need for a jockstrap when a rubber band and a peanut shell would do the trick; how he had two lockermates, skinny Jim Simpson and his own blubber; how the school should charge Mister Lard Ass Stevens extra for soap, given the terrain he had to cover come showertime.

Bucky unshirted the gun, strode to the door, and set its barrel on the window's lower edge, sighting square against the back of Hezel's head. A clink as it touched glass. Hezel turned at the noise and Bucky squeezed the trigger. He glimpsed the burly sinner's blunt brow, his cauliflower nose, the onyx bead of one eye; and then the glass shattered and Hezel's mean black glint turned red, spread outward like burnt film, and Miss Sarah Janeway's noodling trickled to a halt at the tail end of *With the cross of Jeeeee-zus.*

Bucky kicked open the door and leaped over Hezel's still-quivering body. "Freeze, Christian vermin!" he shouted, ready to open up the hot shower of metal tensed in the weapon, but it sounded like somebody else and not quite as committed as Eastwood or Stallone. Besides, his eyes swept the shocked, hymnal-fisted crowd and found young kids, boys of not more than five whose eyes were already lidded with mischief and young girls innocent and whimpery in their pinafores and crinolines, and he knew he had to be selective.

Then the voice slammed in louder and harsher—(KILL THE FUCKERS, BUCKY, KILL THEM SONS OF BITCHES!)—like a new gear ratio kicking in. Bucky used its energy to fight the impulse to relent, dredging up an image of his dead folks fountaining blood like Bucky's Revenge, using that image to sight through as he picked off the Atwoods, four generations of hardware greed on the corner of Main and Garvey: old Grandpappy Andrew, a sneer and a "Shitwad!"

on his withered lips as Bucky stitched a bloody bandoleer of slugs slantwise across his chest; Theodore and Gracia Atwood, turning to protect their young, mowed down by the rude slap of hot metal digging divots of flesh from their faces; their eldest boy Alan, overbearing son of an Atwood who'd shortchanged Bucky on fishhooks last July and whose head and heart exploded as he gestured to his lovely wife Anne, who danced now for them all as her mist-green frock grew red with polkadots; and four-year-old Missy who ran in terror from her bleeding family, ran toward Bucky with a scream curling from her porcelain mouth, her tiny fists raised, staggering into a blast of bullets that lifted her body up with the press of its regard and slammed her back against a splintering pew.

A woman's voice rose through the screams. "Stop him, someone!" she yelled from the front. Bucky pointed toward her voice and let the bullets fly, bloodfucking whole rows of worshippers at one squeeze. Most lay low, cowering out of sight. The suicidal made escape attempts, some running for the doors behind Bucky, others for those up front that led into the pastor's study or back where the choir warmed up. These jackrabbits Bucky picked off, making profane messes out of dark-suited bodies that showed no sense of decorum in their dying, but bled on hard-to-clean church property everywhere he looked.

He eased off the trigger and let the blasts of gun-thunder vanish, though they rang like a sheen of deafness in his ears. "Keep away from the doors!" he shouted, not sure if he could be heard by anyone. It was like talking into fog. "Stay where you are and no one will get hurt," he lied, stepping over dead folk to make his way forward. The crying came to him then, thin and distant, and he saw bodies huddled together as he passed, the wounded and the not-yet-wounded. Call them all what they were, the soon-to-be-deceased.

"Shame on you, Vernon Stevens," came a quavery voice. Bucky looked up. There in the pulpit stood the whey-faced Simon P. Stone, sanctimonious pastor who'd done nothing—his piety deaf to cruelty—to keep Bucky from being the butt of his confirmation class two years before. The knuckles of his thin right hand were white with terror as he clutched, unconscious, a fistful of gilt-edged Bible pages. His surplice hung like a shroud from his taut gaunt shoulders, a tasteful Pontiac gray, sheen and all. A lime-green tippet trailed like an untied tie down the sides of his chest.

"Come down, Satan," said Bucky, hearing sirens in the distance through the bloodpulse of his anger, "come down to the altar and call your flock of demons to you."

"No, Vernon, I won't do that." Pastor Stone's eyes were teary with fear—he of little faith not ready, no not after decades of preaching, to meet his Maker.

Bucky looked around through the sobbing, saw crazed eyes turn away from him, saw between pews the sculpted humps of suited shoulders like blue serge whales stuck in waves, saw—yes! saw Mrs. Irma Wilkins, her red velvet hat a half-shell really with black lace crap on it, her gloved hand dabbing a crumpled hanky to one eye. "Mrs. Wilkins," Bucky said, and her head jerked up like a startled filly, "come here!" Her lids lowered in that snippy way, but she rose, a thin frail stick of a woman, and sidled out of her pew. And as she neared, Bucky was back at the church camp five summers before, out in the woods, holding one end of the crossbranch from which depended the iron kettle, its sole support him and another kid and two badly made and badly sunk Y-shaped branches, and the wind shifted and the smoke of the fire blew like a mask of no-breath into his face and clawed at his eyes no matter how hard he tried to blink past it, and he turned away and let go of the branch saying "My eyes!" and the rude blur that was Irma Wilkins rushed in to catch the branch and to sting him with her condemnation, even now as she approached in this church he could hear her say it, *"Your eyes? OUR STEW!"* as if the fucking food were more important than Bucky's vision and to her it *was* and that voice of hers, that whole put-down attitude reduced Bucky to nothing; but Bucky knew he was something all right, and he saw her pinched little lipless mouth as she came closer, by God it looked like a dotted line and by God he'd oblige her by tearing across it now with his widdle gun, better that than live his whole life hearing this nasty woman's voice reduce him to nothing; and he opened up his rage upon her, rippling across her face with a rain of bullets until her head tore back at the mouth like the top of a Pez dispenser thumbed open, shooting out a stream of crimson coffins, spilling gore down the front of her black dress like cherry liqueur over dark chocolate, and mean Irma Wilkins went down like the worthless sack of shit she was, and Bucky felt damned proud of himself, yes he did, happy campers.

Bucky swung back to Pastor Stone. "Bring 'em all to the front of the church and I won't harm a one of 'em," he said. "But if you refuse, I'll pick 'em off one at a time just like I did Mrs. Wilkins here."

Rest of them had ears. They needed no coaxing, but coaxed instead their whimpering kids out of hiding, out into the aisles and up the red runners to the altar, where Pastor Stone, trembling like unvarnished truth, raised his robed arms as if in benediction, as if he were posing for a picture, Pastor Simon P. Stone and his bleating sheep.

The muffled squawk of a bullhorn turned Bucky's head to a tall unstained window at his left. A squat man in blue stood on the grass at the near edge of the parking lot, legs planted firmly apart, elbows bent, face and hands obliterated by a black circle. "Vernon Stevens," came his humorless voice, "lay down your weapon and come out with your hands raised. We will not harm you if you do as I say. We have the church surrounded. Repeat. The church. Is. Surrounded." The bullhorn squawked off and the black circle came down so that Bucky could see clearly the ain't-I-a-big-boy-now, pretend courage painted on the man's face. Glancing back, Bucky saw bobbing blue heads through the two small squares of window that let onto the narthex, a scared rookie or two, the long stems of assault rifles jostling like shafts of wheat in a summer breeze.

Doubt crept into him. And fear. His finger eased off the trigger. Tension began to drain from his arms.

FINISH THE JOB! came the voice, like a balloon fist suddenly inflating inside his skull, pressing outward as if to burst bone. *LOOK AT THEM, BUCKY! LOOK AND*

67

REMEMBER WHAT THEY'VE DONE TO YOU!

And Bucky looked. And Bucky saw. There was Bad Sam in his Sunday best, frog-faced pouting young tough, a lick of light brown hair laid across his brow, freckles sprayed on his bloated cheeks, Bad Sam who'd grabbed Bucky off his bike when Bucky was nine, slammed him to the cement of the sidewalk by Mr. Murphy's house and slapped his face again and again until his cheeks bruised and bled. And through his tears, he could see Mr. Murphy at his front window, withdrawing in haste at being discovered; Mr. Murphy who'd always seemed so kind, tending his tulip beds as Bucky biked by, and now here he was in church along with his tiny wife and their daughter Patricia in a white dress and a round brimmed hat that haloed her head. And next to her stood Alex Menche, a gas jockey at the Exxon station, corner of First and Main, whose look turned to hot ice whenever Bucky walked by, who never blinked at him, never talked to him, but just stared, oily rag in hand, jaw moving, snapping a wad of gum. And back behind Alex he caught a glimpse of Mr. Green the janitor, who'd yelled at the lunchbox crowd in second grade to Shut up! even when their mouths were busy with peanut butter. And odd Elvira Freeborn, New Falls' weirdo-lady, who laid claim in good weather to a corner of the city park across from the town hall and had conversation with anyone who chanced by and lingered there—even weirdo Elvira had come up to him one day when he'd been desperate enough for company to go seek her out, had come up all smiles, her hair wispy gray and twisting free of its bun, and said, "My, my, Vernon, you are one fat ugly thing, yes you are, and if you were mine, I'd sew your mouth shut, I would; by God I'd starve that flab right off your bones and I'd see about getting you a nose job for that fat knob of a honker you got on your face and—" on and on and on, and now her eyes were on him here in church, off-yellow glaring cat's-eyes like a reformed witch having second thoughts. And beside her was Sarah Janeway the organist, who'd laughed and then tried to hide it when Bucky auditioned for the children's choir at the age of eight, a no-talent bitch with her wide vacant eyes encircled in wide glasses rimmed in thin red and her hair cropped short as her musical gifts and her absurd flowered dress poking out of the shimmering-green choir robe down below, and she was standing there white-faced and whiny, and then the bullhorn bullshit started up again, and Bucky brought his one true friend up to his chest and let the surge of righteous wrath seize him.

He made them dance, every last one of them.

He played the tune. They tripped and swayed to the rhythm of his song. Wounds opened like whole notes in them. Sweeping glissandos of gore rose up like prayers of intercession.

Behind him he felt a flood of cops rush in to pick up the beat and join him, to judder and jolt the music out of *him* with music of their own. Bucky, tripped out on giving back in spades what New Falls had so unstintingly bestowed upon him over the years, turned about to spray death into the boys in blue at his back. But there were too many of them, and a goodly number were already in position, rifles beaded on him.

Then pain seized his right knee and danced up his leg in small sharp steps, like invisible wasps landing on him, fury out. Needles of fire watusied across his belly. Two zigzags of lead staggered up the ladders of his ribs and leaped for Bucky's head. Something impossible to swallow punched through his teeth, filling his mouth with meat and blood.

And then his brain lit up like a second sun and all the pain winked out. The terrible thunder of weaponry put to use went away, only to be replaced by organ music so sweet it made Bucky want to wet his pants and not give a good goddamn about the consequences.

He felt himself drift apart like a dreamer becoming someone else. The cops froze, caught in mid-fire. About him, the church walls roiled and wowed like plaster turned to smoke. But it wasn't smoke. It was mist, fog, clouds. They billowed down into the church, rolling and shifting and swirling among the corpses. Bucky glanced back at the altar, saw the bodies of his victims posed in attitudes of death, saw Pastor Simon P. Stone, his robed arms out in crucifixion, veed at the waist as if he'd just caught the devil's medicine ball in his belly.

69

But right behind Bucky, close enough to startle him, was his own body, bits of flesh being torn out like tufts of grass at a driving range, shoots of blood looking like hopeful red plants just coming into sunlight. He circled, by willing it, about his body, feeling the cumulus clouds cotton under his feet, soothing his soles, as he gazed in astonishment at his head, pate cracked open all round like the top of an eggshell, hovering a foot above the rest of it in a spray of blood and brain. He reached out, touched the stray piece of skull, tried to force it back in place, but it was as if it were made of stone and cemented for all eternity to the air. Likewise the freshets of gore issuing like bloody thoughts from his brain, which, though not cold, were as stiff as icicles.

The music swelled, recaptured his attention. Looking about for its source, he saw emerge from each tiny cloud a creature, all in white, all of white and gold, delicate of hand, beatific of face, and every one of them held a thing of curves in its hands. Their angel mouths O'd like moon craters. Thin fingers swept in blizzards of beauty across iridescent harps. And yet their music was neither plucked nor sung, but a pain-pure hymn rolling out in tones richer than any man-made organ.

They made the bloody scene beautiful, sanctifying it with their psalm. And now their bodies swerved as though hinged and they raised their eyes to the dioramic massacre before the altar and up past the huge golden cross even to the white plaster ceiling above it, beyond which the spire lofted heavenward. With a great groan, as if angelic eyes could move mountains with a look, the top of the building eased open, sliding outward on invisible runners to hang there in the open air. And down into the church descended a great blocky bejeweled thing, an oblong Spielbergian UFO Bucky thought at first. But then he saw the sandals, the feet, the robes, the hands gripping firmly the arms of the throne like Abe Lincoln, the chest bedecked in white, and the great white beard, and he guessed what he was in for.

But when the head came fully into view, Bucky had to laugh. Like Don Rickles trapped in a carpet, the face of an angry black woman grimaced out from behind the white beard and mustache of God. Her cheeks puffed out like wet sculpted obsidian, her dark eyes glared, and just in front of a Hestonian sweep of white hair, a tight black arch of curls hugged her face like some dark rider's chaps curving about the belly of his steed. The white neck of the deity was stiff and rigid, as if locked in a brace.

"Bucky Stevens," She boomed, Her eyes moving from him to a space of air in front of Her, "you'd best be getting yourself up here this instant, you hear?"

"Yes, ma'm," he said, drifting around his exploding corpse and sailing up over the bloody crowd at the altar. He could still sense how fat he was, but he felt as light and unplodding as a sylph. "You sending me to hell?" he asked.

She laughed. "Looks to Me like you found your *own* way there." Her eyes surveyed the carnage. "First off, young man, I want to say I 'preciate what you did for Me. I like sinners who listen to My suggestions and have the balls to carry them out."

"That was *You*?"

"Does God lie?"

"No, ma'm."

"Damn right He don't, and I'm God, so you just shove those doubts aside and listen up."

"Um, scuse me, ma'm," said Bucky, shuffling his feet in the air, "but how come God's a black woman? I mean in Sunday school, we never—"

"God ain't a black woman, Mister Bucky, leastways no more He ain't. He's been that for a while, oh 'bout three weeks or so." She smiled suddenly. "But now He gets to be a fat white boy named Bucky Stevens."

Bucky brightened. He didn't doubt for a moment what She'd said. He couldn't. It speared like truth into his heart. "You mean I get to . . . to take over? There's no punishment for killing all these people?"

God chuckled, a high-pitched woo-wee kind of sound. "That ain't what I said a-tall." She did a stiff-necked imitation of a headshake as She spoke.

Bucky was mystified: "I don't get it."

God leaned forward like She had a board strapped to Her back. "I'll be brief," She said, "just so's you can hustle your fat butt up here quicker and let Me come down and do My dying. I killed me a whole officeload of people three weeks ago, got blown away by a security guard after I hosed those heartless fuckers at Century 21. Same sorta miracle that's happening to you now, happened to me then. Only God was this unhinged lunatic I'd seen on Dan Rather the week before, some nut who went to O'Hare and picked off ground crew and passengers not lucky enough to be going through one of those tubes. He got blown away too, became God, then talked me into wiping out my co-workers when they gave me the axe. So I did it, and coaxed you along same's he did me, and here we are."

The music was doing beautiful things to Bucky's mind. He grew very excited. "You mean I'm going to be in charge of everything? I can make any changes I feel like making, I can stop all the misery if I want to?" God ummm-hmmmed. "But why would anyone, why would *You*, want to give that up?"

She looked agitated, like She wanted to laugh and cry and holler all at the same time. Instead She said, "As My momma used to say, young Master Stevens, experience is the best teacher a body can have." She glared at him suddenly and Bucky felt himself swept forward and up.

He windmilled his arms, struggling to find his center of gravity, but found himself fluttering and turning like an autumn leaf, tumbling spout over teakettle toward the great black face, toward the crazy brown eyes. He headed straight between them, fearing he'd smash on the browbone, but instead doubled and split like a drunkard's vision and fell and swelled into the black pools of God's pupils. In the blink of an eye, he inflated. That's how it felt to him, like his head felt when they stuck his arm and taped it down, knocking him out for an ingrown toenail operation when he was ten, only all over his body this time and he didn't lose consciousness. He unlidded his eyes just in time to see the stocky black woman wink at him before she put her hands together as if in prayer, sang out "So long, sucker!" and swan-dived into his shattering body.

Bucky gazed about at the angels on their clouds and felt guy-wires coming from their O'd mouths as if He were a Macy's Day balloon and they the marching guardians who kept Him from floating free. The throne rose slowly and the angels with it. Bucky took His first Godbreath and felt divine. Like Captain Kirk, He was in command now, He sat at the helm, and things by God were going to fly right from here on out.

But then, as He lifted above the church and its roof clicked into place, time unfroze and, with it, the pain of those inside. He felt it all, like a mailed fist slamming into His solar plexus again and again: Simon Stone, small and mean inside like a mole, gasping for one final breath; Sarah Janeway, two months pregnant, trying in vain to hold back the rope-spill of her intestines; kind-hearted Elvira Freeborn, in so many ways the sanest person there, who let her dying fall over her like a new sun dress, a thing of razor and flame. And even the dead—Coach Hezel, the Atwoods, Irma Wilkins and the rest—even from these, Bucky felt the echoes of their suffering and, transcending time, seeped into their dying a thousand times over.

And then He rose over New Falls, did Bucky Stevens, feeling His holy tendrils reach into everyone that wept and wandered there. He knew at last the torment of his parents and the riches they'd lost inside themselves, and it made His heart throb with pain. Bucky rose, and, in rising, sank into every hurting soul in town, spreading Himself thick everywhere. And all was painful clarity inside Him. It grew and crackled, the misery, and still He rose and sank, moving like Sherwin-Williams paint to engulf the globe, seeping deep down into the earth. Bucky wanted to scream. And scream He did. And His scream was the cause, and the sound, of human misery.

He tried to bring His hands to His face. To puncture His eardrums. To thumb out His eyes. But they clung like mules to the hard arms of the throne, not budging, and His eyelids would not shut, and His earflaps sucked all of it in like maelstroms of woe. Pockets of starvation flapped open before Him like cover stories blown, and each death-eyed Ethiopian became unique to Him—the clench of empty stomachs, the wutter and wow of dying minds.

Like dental agony, layer beneath layer surprising one at the untold depths of it, Bucky's pain intensified and spread, howling and spiraling off in all directions. And after a while, it didn't exactly dull, nor did He get used to it, but rather He rose to meet it, to yield to it as the storm-tossed seafarer gives up the struggle and moves into the sweep of the sea. He was the pincushion of pain, He was the billions of screaming pins, He was the billions of thumbs pressing them down into flannel. He suffered all of it, and knew Himself to be the cause of it all. Caught in the weave, He *was* the weave.

He almost smiled, it was so perverse; but the smile was ripped from His face by new outrage. There seemed no end to the torment, no end to burgeoning pain. As soon as He thought He'd hit bottom, the bottom fell out. He began to wonder if the black woman had lied to Him, if maybe He was trapped in this nightmare for all eternity. While He watched with eyes that could not close, new births killed young girls, new deaths tore at mourners, new forms of woe were kennel-bred and unleashed. Bucky was fixed in His firmament, and all was hell with the world.

Plunged down the slippery slope of despair, He cast His great eyes about, sought for pustules of resentment, found them. The seeds of His redemption they were, these seething souls. The black woman—Miriam Jefferson Jones—had, like her predecessor, been nursing others along, and now Bucky reached out to them and took up the whisper in their ears, the whisper momentarily stilled at the shift in deity. Heavens yes, Sean Flynn, he assured the young man leaned against the stone wall, huddled with his mates, it's only proper you elbow under their fuckin' transport at night, fix old Mother Flammable there, crawl the hell out o' there, give it the quick plunge, watch all them limey bastards kiss the night sky over Belfast with their bones. And yes, Alicia Condon of Lost Nation, Iowa, it's okay to take your secret obsession with the purity of the newborn to its limit, it is indeed true that if you could wipe out a whole nursery of just-delivered infants before they hit that fatal all-corrupting second day of life, the Second Coming of My Own Sweet Son would indeed be swiftly upon the sinning race of mankind. And yes, oh most decidedly yes, Gopal Krishnan and Vachid Dastjerdi and Moshe Naveh, you owe it to your respective righteous causes to massacre whole busloads, whole airports, whole towns full of enemy flesh.

There were oodles of them walking the earth, ticking timebombs, and all of them He tended and swayed that way, giving with a whisper gentle nudges and shoves toward mass annihilation. New ones too, promising buds of bitterness, Bucky began to cultivate. Some one of them was certain to bloom any moment now—oh God, how Bucky prayed to Himself for it to be soon—at least one brave quarterback on this playing field of sorrow was sure to snatch that ball out of the sky and run for all he was worth, pounding cleat against turf, stiff-arming those who dared try to block him, not stopping till he crossed the forbidden line and slammed that bleeding pigskin down in triumph.

That was the hope, through agonies untold, that kept Bucky going. That was the hope that made things hum.

FRUCTUS IN EDEN

Cringing naked and ashamed in the bushes, they could hear above the hammering of their hearts the dread rud and thumble of His footfall. Guilty as sin they were, thought Adam; as guilty as the fruit had been good.

Yet, though in the foulest depths of fear and remorse the first father cowered, even so, half-pendulous with new cravings was he, squatting there thigh to thigh beside the long-tressed Eve, his "beloved lovecunt" as he called her in their moments of dalliance (for in the first days, that word held no pejorative, but partook rather of the sensual beauty inherent in words like "zephyr" or "stream"), those precious moments when they lay together on beds of moss in the full perfection of the sun.

But now the sky roiled with storm clouds, and useless knowledge clouded their brains. The Serpent had done his damnedest, their incisors had wantonly penetrated the taut fruitskin, and they'd torn, tongued, chewed, and swallowed the bitter pulp of divine wisdom. Now had come the moment to pay for their disobedience.

"Where are you?" He boomed from everywhere, feigning ignorance. The swish of His robes against the tall grass struck terror in them. Then, they beheld as though draped over spirit the sandaled feet of God, His holy ankles, the hem of His robes, the towering majesty of Him, and lofted far above the trees His face, a face of patience and love and the terrible indifference of divinity. His beard was full and off-white, like

76

tinged fleece. His eyes shown at once ancient and newborn. Upon His brow, the crown dazzled.

Adam took Eve's hand. Together they rose and quitted the refuge of the underbrush, falling to their knees and humbling themselves before Him. Adam felt his tumescence deferentially shrivel to near nothing.

"My children," came the heartrending voice of their Maker, "lift up your eyes and look at Me." They did so, feeling their souls cringe within. His eyes brimmed with betrayal. "Did I not leave you free and unfettered in this delightful paradise, free to wander where you would, to give names to My creations, and to conjoin with all the abandon appropriate to creatures in the perfect enjoyment of their carnality?"

"You did, Lord," mumbled the first couple.

"And did I not suffer you to satisfy your natural craving for food with the fruit of any tree in the garden, any of the thousand trees that spill over so profusely with fruit which, until this moment, knew neither how to overripen nor to spoil?"

"All but one, Lord," they said, feeling like specks of shit beneath his sandals.

"Yes, all but one. That one tree in whose shade you now kneel, the tree that bestows the knowledge of Good and Evil. The fruit of this tree only did I deny you, and you agreed willingly and with good cheer never to eat of it."

"We did, Lord."

God's words were thick with sorrow: "Why then have you disobeyed Me?"

Adam looked at Eve, Eve looked at Adam.

Then began the recriminations, choking the air like flames in a furnace. Adam blasted Eve; Eve tore into the Serpent; neither thought to blame themselves. Their guilt gave way to anger, their anger to sorrowful repentance and pleas for clemency, and thence to silence, the silence of a prisoner watching his judge's lips slide, syllable by syllable, along a sentence of death.

Once more their knees sank to the dust and their gaze fell past their genitals. Adam's penis drooped earthward, shedding one sad tear of pre-ejaculate. No more would he bury his mouth in Eve's bush, no more feel her tongue upon his testicles, no more cup her delectable breasts as she straddled him and melted her labia about his manhood.

And God said, "I ought to smite you. I should strike you down where you kneel, take back your heartbeats, suck out your breath, lay waste your limbs, and pulverize your bones even unto the marrow. However. There are times in this universe when justice must yield to mercy. And as I know that, because you truly believed Me full of wrath and all unbending, your repentance was sincere, I shall, this one time, spare your lives."

Doubting his ears, Adam looked up. A beatific smile hung from God's lips. "Let us forget, My children, that this ever came to pass. Promise never again to partake of the fruit of this tree, and I shall wipe the slate clean."

Adam, though stunned, seized the moment. Helping his wife up, he said, "Dear sweet Lord, we give Thee bounteous thanks." Eve stammered out her gratitude as well. Her fair face looked blasted as by a great wind, Adam thought, wrapping an arm about her waist and gripping her hand.

And God laughed a rich, fruity laugh that washed away their terror. By the time He dismissed them with a wave of His hand, turned on His heel, and moved away, brushing the treetops with His robes, our first parents too had caught God's laugh in their throats, feeling it reach up into their skulls and down through every limb and organ. Still frantic with laughter, they joined genitals and fucked the storm clouds, the rest of the day, and much of the evening away. If they paused to feast, it was more often upon each other than upon some luscious piece of fruit freely plucked from one licit tree limb or another.

So at last they sank, stuck flesh to flesh, into the deep sleep of those who have transgressed and somehow, but who can say how, gotten away with it.

Morning sun upon her belly. Slither of an erection moving up one thigh. Eve winked an eye open and gazed past her golden breasts, fully expecting Adam, finding instead the dry wrinkled skin of the Serpent exciting her. In the distance, Adam gloried in the dawn, his arms raised to a brilliant sky.

"Quite a hunk, your hubby."

She sighed. "Yes, he is." Then, remembering, Eve's face raged: "Listen, snake, you have a little explaining to do. Your smooth-tongued arguments in favor of eating the forbidden fruit nearly got us killed."

"Killed?" The Serpent recoiled and hissed a smile. "You don't look dead to me, my dear. Quite the contrary. You look deliciously alive, good enough to eat, decidedly succulent, something to sink one's teeth into."

"Dream on," she said, and rolled over, tossing her hair behind her. She plucked a tall blade of grass and placed it between her lips.

Insinuating itself onto a flat rock near her right shoulder, the Serpent coiled, watching warily the first mother's face. "Just as I imagined," it said. "Eating from the tree has given you a thoughtful air you lacked before. It's really quite fetching."

Eve grunted and looked away.

"You may not know this—it's something I didn't tell you yesterday, since, if I may be candid for a moment, I fully expected God to banish you from Eden—but the more fruit you eat from that tree, the wiser you'll grow. And the more lovely you'll become not only in your husband's eyes, but in the eyes of man and beast alike."

She whipped her head around. "Save it. We're wise to you, me and Adam. Yesterday we barely escaped with our lives. But we've learned our lesson. From now on, we'll tend that tree, but we're not going near the fruit."

The Serpent shook its sad head, clucking its tongue. Looking past Eve, it saw Adam turn toward his mate, noted the concern on the first father's face at the sight of her tempter, watched him sprint toward them. "Still, you must admit it's a lovely taste, a taste one really oughtn't to do without. And where once forgiveness comes, my lovely, who's to say it won't come again?"

The Serpent had more on its mind, but Adam's rough hands reached down and fisted its tail, hefted it into the air, swung it like a heavy weight thrice round his head, and let it fly deep into the outlying thickets of Eden.

"Good riddance to bad rubbish," said Adam, "to coin a phrase. Whatever coins might be."

Eve gazed thoughtfully up at the tree. "Adam," she said, her eyes coming to light on the tantalizing fruit, "I've been thinking."

The second time, He was angrier than they'd ever seen Him. Into the garden He swept, riding upon a whirlwind. His hair was tempest-tossed, His eyes flashed fire. "Down on your knees!" He trumpeted, blasting their ears. "Nay, flat on your bellies, you miserable excuses for humanity!"

Adam pressed his belly into the dirt, arms thrust out before him. Groveling washed like balm over his soul. He was amazed how sensuous the earth felt along the length of his body. No wonder the Serpent warped and wriggled from place to place, he thought. He stole a peek at Eve, who was stretched out beside him, her long hair atumble down her shoulders, her breast-mounds bulging out beneath, lovely as all of her. Adam wondered, as his flesh began to weave and grow beneath him, if this would be his last vision before death swallowed them up.

"Cease your vile thoughts, O miserable man, and heed the words of your Maker."

God He sounded pissed.

"By all rights, I ought to end your lives at once. It's clear that neither of you is capable of obedience to any law I lay down. Set up a barrier, turn My back, and you'll scratch and claw to be the first to o'erleap it!"

Thunder blasted them flat. Lightning rent the earth not six yards from their heads. They cried out in terror. Across their backs, a cold, drenching rain juddered down. "Yes, be fearful, My poor dear creatures. And repentant. For these raindrops are the tears of God, My tears, shed for what I must now most reluctantly do."

"Mercy, dear Father," sobbed Adam. "Mercy upon Your sinning children. Grievously have I sinned, choosing yet again to disobey You and eat of the fruit. Take my life, if You must. But spare the gentle Eve, whom I convinced to taste what she should not have tasted."

Then Eve spoke up, protesting that she alone was at fault, that her husband was blameless in all things save in taking her blame upon himself.

While his wife spoke, Adam raised his chin and peered through the rain at God's sandals. He shut his eyes in disbelief, then reopened them. It was true. The divine Maker, though He still dwarfed them, had diminished in stature since His last visit. His big toe, which before had come up to their chests as they knelt, now rose no higher than their prostrate heads.

God rocked upon His heels, hands clenched behind His back. The silence that had fallen between Him and his recalcitrant creatures was broken only by the noise of His incoherent fuming and muttering.

Adam knew their lives hung in the balance.

Abruptly the rocking stopped. "Get up!" He boomed at them. And up they got. Craning his neck, Adam stared into God's index finger, which stabbed like death through the Edenic air. "One more chance," came the raging voice. "One more. That's all you get. If you so much as squint at that tree the wrong way, it's over."

Trembling to the bone, Adam looked into the fiery eyes of God and did not blink, though the blast of divine rage seared his face and threatened blindness. When the Holy of Holies stormed off at last, red and green blotches danced in the sight of Adam.

Now when the Serpent returned, Adam, wiser than his years, brought him into their deliberations. For hours they weighed alternatives, debated issues of freedom and slavery, mapped out and discarded grand strategies.

In the midst of one of Adam's perorations, Eve cut him off with a simple "Husband." She pointed up into the branches of the tree. "I'm hungry. For that."

The Serpent looked at Adam.

Adam raised an eyebrow.

Then, setting all thought aside, they all three did the inevitable. In the blink of an eye, they fell upon that tree like bees on blossoms, like lawyers on mishap, like vultures on dead men's flesh.

The Serpent, having eaten more than his fill, belched and said, "I'll get the tools." With a groan, he slid his great bulk along the ground and was gone.

Adam and Eve, too consumed with gluttony to care what their friend had meant, stuffed themselves with succulent fruit. Breathing became secondary, and for a time, their world consisted of naught but plucking, biting, chewing, swallowing, and plucking again. When they grew weary of feeding themselves, they fed each other. Eve crammed the juicy pulp past Adam's incisors. Adam shoved fruit down Eve's gullet with all the fervor of a cunt-hungry stud pressing home his fuckflesh. They stuffed themselves, our first parents, like there was no tomorrow.

As they gorged and grew great, the tree of knowledge lost its every fruit and leaf. Like the arms of a beggar seeking raiment, it lofted its bare limbs into the perfect air of Eden. But its leaves now blanketed the ground and its fruit ballooned the bellies of the insatiate sinners, bloating their bodies beyond all reasonable bound.

Adam's hand, animate with desire, went organ-hunting among Eve's rolls of flab, and Eve's among Adam's. But finding lust within gluttony proved no easy task and they had to make do with blubbery hugs instead. It was in the midst of one such clumsy clench that Eve heard hoofbeats mild and meek and saw, over her husband's left shoulder, God riding toward them upon a squat, gray, four-legged animal whose name eluded her.

Adam gave a low whistle. "Divine creator," he said, "you seem to have shrunk a good deal. You're just about human-sized, I'd say. If anything, you're quite a bit leaner about the middle than we are."

"What happened to you?" asked Eve, astonished.

God just looked at them, sad-eyed. He slipped off his donkey and sandals, let fall his robes, dug beads of blood from his brow with a crown of thorns. Draped about his waist, falling from hip to hip like a cotton grimace, a simple loincloth concealed his godhood. He leaned back against the barren tree, crossed his legs, stretched out his arms, and rose along the rough bark nearly three feet into the air. Left and right, from shoulder to hand, his arms traced the contours of the tree's bifurcating limbs. His eyes were wet with sorrow.

Rage filled fat Adam. Each breath became an effort. "Come down from there and punish us, you miserable excuse for divinity! We did it a third time, Eve and I. We ate until there was nothing left. One last binge, that's all we wanted. No remorse, just a final feast and then sweet oblivion. Now get down here and mete out justice!"

But God only fixed his fat son with a simple look of compassion and spoke not a word.

Adam's jowls trembled. His puffy hands flexed and clenched. He became vaguely aware of the Serpent's huge bulk swaying first to one side, then the other, putting heavy objects into his hands. A hammer. A cold fistful of spikes. Beneath his feet he felt the moving green of leaves and then he'd leaped to the lower branches of the tree and was pounding spiteful iron into his maker's left palm, straight through into treelimb. Before God's right hand, Eve's hammer swung wide, broke the deity's pinkie, then drove her spike home in two swift strokes. Good lord she was fat, thought Adam, seeing her beauty shine forth even through folds of pudge.

Together they pierced the feet. A simple task, this piercing, yet it drew them closer. With each hammer blow, their love augmented. Crucifixion, they discovered, when performed upon scapegoat deities, can often be a powerful aphrodisiac. God's blood beribboned his feet and dripped from his toes. Where it fell, Calvary clover grew.

Stepping back hand in hand with his spouse to admire their craft, Adam watched Eve's breasts rise and fall with excitement. A rampant hunger seemed to seize her as she fixed her eyes on their impaled creator. She relinquished Adam's grasp and moved forward. Then she snaked one hand beneath the simple swatch of cloth and undraped it from God's body, exposing his sex.

Adam gaped in awe at the size of him. Maybe it was the light, he thought. He took a step closer. Nope. No trick of sun or shadow. This was one huge tool, dangling now from a dying deity. A tragic waste, in his opinion, of progenitive flesh.

Eve, however, clearly saw one last use for it. She hefted the organ in her hands, ran her fingers along its underside, got it to grow bigger still. Then she wrapped her jaws around it like a python, gorging her fat face.

Around the clearing, in the center of which grew the now-barren tree, animals made their silent approach. The graceful heads of two gazelles peered round the flanks of an elephant, who stood, gray-eyed and baggy, looking on in puzzlement. Birds of every shape and color perched in the surrounding trees, their songs stilled, their heads cocked to one side. Upon the ground, serpents slithered, insects danced closer, squirrels and ferrets and martens and rats leaped over one another and darted in to freeze and stare. The circle of beasts hung there, dumb and attentive.

In his loins Adam could feel all nature stirring. He watched Eve feast upon her maker. Her swollen arms barely bent at the elbows. Her chubby fingers could hardly close around the cock of the crucified lord. He saw the spread of her legs, the beads of moisture on her pubic hair, the exquisite anus playing hide and seek with him as her butt-cheeks writhed.

He'd never had that anus, never particularly wanted it until now. But now it drew his every attention, closed out all other sights, urged his feet forward. Nestling his manhood between her buttocks, he touched his cocktip to the tight centerpoint. Eve, without ceasing her oral ministrations, swiveled her hips to signal her consent to Adam's penetration. Adam spat on his palms, slicked along the length of his erection, and eased into the depths of his beloved wife's derriere.

Eve leaned against God's womanly thighs. She could feel his balls tighten toward orgasm. His pre-ejaculate oozed free and gradual into her mouth, delighting beyond measure her taste buds. Between her cheeks, back where things grew narrow, she could feel her husband fill her full to gasping with his erect flesh.

And now, coiling up her left leg came the Serpent. She supposed he'd stop and speak to her, perhaps egg her on. Instead he parted the pink petals of her womanhood and began to fuck her with his head. Glancing down, she saw the slick, criss-crossed snakeskin move rhythmically in and out of her, coated now with her lovejuice.

Eve felt deliriously stuffed. God's crimped thatch tickled against her forehead like the gentle brush of a breeze. His tool tasted like the cock of all creativity on her tongue. Down below, lesser life forms pulsed out their polyrhythms, readying fecund liquids.

In at her ears now crept the murmurings of nature, until then silent with reverence. Now there was growing excitement in the air. Rising to voracious receptivity, drawing her three seminarians up to a mindless frenzy of seed-spilling, Eve heard all nature twitter and roar and rustle in sympathy.

Almost there now.

Almost home.

Then the floodgates burst on all fronts at once. Her husband bit into her shoulder and juiced her from behind. The Serpent, rippling from tail to head, vomited gobbets of forbidden fruit into her womb. And from the sides of her mouth, gouts of godsperm gushed, so voluminous was the deity's discharge, so impossible the task of swallowing it all.

The fluids roiled inside her, coming together at her very core. Up she swelled, backing off from the tree and squeezing Adam and the Serpent out of her. Inside she was all generation. She could feel the teeming zygotes spring and swirl within, latching onto bone and organ, tapping into spirit, jittering through ontogeny like manic nuns fingering rosaries, like prayer wheels gone wild.

As she blimped up, her lungs drew in air unceasing. Just when it seemed that inhalation might be Eve's eternal curse, the gates of Eden burst open outward, and screams and infants began to shoot forth from her. Bright balls of every color they were, these kids. Out they flew, slick with vernix and hugging their afterbirths to them. Red ones, green ones, black and brown and orange ones; some as clear as glass, all shades conceivable and many that were not. Through the lips of her quim and out the gates of Eden they spun and tumbled, scattered by the winds of chance hither and yon over the earth to flourish or starve at destiny's whim.

When the grand exodus was over and the last humanoid hopeful—deep purple and no thicker than a thumb—zinged out of Eve and careered off who knew where, she lay there steeped in sweat and panting with exultation. Eve was fat no more, but restored to svelte. So, she noted, was Adam, whose outpouring of spunk had spent in the exertion his store of blubber. He helped her to her feet and gave her a round, resounding hug.

"Time to go, honey," he said.

She nodded, looked down, hesitated. Then, to the Serpent, wrapped round the base of the tree: "You coming with us?"

"No thanks, pretty one," he said. "My place is with him." He slipped into God's fundament, coiled inside his large intestine (whose length he matched perfectly), and fell asleep for all eternity.

Above, head snapped back from collarbone loll, God roared in anguish.

Adam took Eve by the hand, smiled, and led her toward the open gates. "The world's our oyster, Eve. What say we have it on the half-shell?"

She held back. "What about God?"

"We're beyond all that now, you and me," he scoffed. "Let our progeny create deities if they must. As for us, I think secular humanism suits us better."

"Ugh, that sounds dreadful," Eve objected. "If we're going to call ourselves something, let it be something we can feel proud of, something with a ring to it."

"Such as?"

"I don't know. Let's see." She thought a moment, then brightened. "How about sacred universalists?"

"Sacred what?"

"Universalists," said Eve, warming to it. "Because absolutely everything we see and know and touch or even think or fantasize about is shot through and through with the awful light of divinity."

Adam smiled bitterly. "Everything but this green mausoleum we've been cooped up in." He gestured, like a man gone mad, about the Earthly Paradise. In this fallen world of ours, dear reader, the life of every human male demands its adamantine core of resentment, its refusal to forgive, the galling pill stuck eternally in its proud male throat. Adam found his in Eden, hung on a tree and suffering clear to the walls. "Come on, Eve. Let's go find our sons and daughters."

Eve nodded, her eyes lowered. But the aftertaste of God hung like temptation upon her tongue.

"Don't leave me," came his agonized whisper.

Pausing at the gates, Adam frowned up at the tree. Then he cocked his head toward the animals, watched them gallop and slither and lope and lumber past him, and slammed the gates of Eden shut with a resounding clang. The echo rang in Eve's ears long after Eden dropped below the horizon, and the vision of her lord's twisted limbs hung tantalizingly before her inner eye.

Much later, when she'd had her fill of Adam, Eve set off on her own to regain Eden. And yet, though she looked ever and anon with a light heart and a hopeful mien, her search, in the end, proved fruitless.

ONE FLESH:
A CAUTIONARY TALE

We admit it. There's a right way and a wrong way to bring one's loving lady into conformity with the image of womanly perfection that burns bright in every man's heart. Dad and me, we went about it the wrong way. That's clear to us now, after all the grief that came pelting down into our lives when half the Sacramento police force jackbooted their way through our front door and kept us from further satisfying our desires, modest as they were, on the naked limbs of our composite wife.

But it's our feeling that before the state—that vast motherless bastion of rectitude and righteousness—unlocks our cell to dead-march us along its sexless corridor, then to mumble piety into us from the mercy-thin pages of its Holy Bible, cinch us down snug and secure, and hiss open its gas jets to pack us off to the next life, we owe it to the rest of you idolatrous cockwielders out there to pass on the lesson we learned. Does that sound agreeable to you, Dad? Dad, I'm talking to you! He says it does.

It began with a birth, nearly nineteen years ago, on the night of February 15th, 1970. My dear wife Rhonda was all of twenty-one then, amber of eye and huge of breast, vivacious, fun-loving, ever faithful to me in spite of my shortcomings and the handful of cunt-hungry mongrels that always seemed to be sniffing about her skirts. Lovely as life itself was Rhonda, and carrying our son.

My folks came down from Chico in mid-January to help with last-minute preparations; they were radiant with love for us both and just itching to be grandparents. Rhonda's mother, Wilma Flannery, flew in from Iowa to be with "her precious baby" in her finest hour. She was one eccentric biddy, my mother-in-law, old and wizened at fifty. Her husband had left her soon after Rhonda was born, never to be heard from again. That didn't surprise me and I don't think it surprised Rhonda either. Although I wished Wilma had stayed in Oskaloosa, I did my level best to ignore her high-pitched demands and irritating ways and focus all my attention on Rhonda.

My wife's projected delivery date was Washington's Birthday, and around a quiet dinner one night at Mario's, my mom and especially my dad—Oh come off it, Dad, you know you did!—teased us about it, threatening to call their grandchild George or Georgina in honor of the man on the dollar. Rhonda's mother sat hunched over her plate, wolfing down tortellini. Good food always seemed to shut dear old Wilma up for a while.

As it happened, the baby arrived ahead of schedule. On the afternoon of the 15th, Rhonda and the two older women, wanting some girl-time alone, talked me and Dad into a night on the town. Before they booted us out into the light drizzle that had begun to come down, I pinned a hastily scrawled itinerary on the kitchen corkboard, just in case: dinner and drinks at California Fats, then a late-night showing of *Psycho* at the Tower. Dad and I were fond of Hitchcock movies back then. And after the accident that brought us together, we loved them even more.

The call came halfway through dinner. We'd done more drinking than eating, a lot more. Three swallows of wine to every forkful of food, I'd guess. Ordinarily we'd have thought twice about taking to the highway with that much alcohol in our veins. But I was determined to be right there by Rhonda's side when my baby was born, and judging from Mom's babbling over the phone from the hospital, we had no time to waste thinking about what was safe and what wasn't. So we threw some bills on the table, staggered together to my VW van, ramped up onto Highway 50, and five minutes later—in a passing maneuver that would have meant certain death at high noon on a bone-dry road with a teetotaling priest behind the wheel—we rammed into the back end of a screeching Raley's truck and felt for one mercifully brief instant the twin agonies of metal-mangled flesh and bone from the front and the whomp and sizzle of a fireball engulfing us from the rear.

If the notations of the hospital staff present at my son's delivery were correct, our precise time of death was 7:41 p.m. There was tightness everywhere and a painful sliding and then suddenly the chill of freedom. We were somehow nakedly intertwined, my dad and I. When the shock of the cold was blanketed away and sweet warm milk filled our mouth and soothed our belly, we bleared open our eyes and were astounded to see a gigantic Rhonda-face beaming down at us. We tried to call out to her, but our mouth was full of nipple and our body throbbed and the blankets felt so warm and cozy around us that we soon drifted off. When we awoke, nothing but baby sounds came out of us, no matter how carefully we tried to speak. When Dad saw his wife Arlene (my mom) smiling down at us, I couldn't help but feel his sadness and his frustration, and we wailed with our whole being and fisted our tiny fists and did our best to squeeze every cubic inch of air out of our little lungs with each scream. But just when we thought merciful death might reclaim us, the air came rushing back in and the cruel joke continued.

Our name was Jason. I'd picked it out myself, not because it was popular—the J-names were only starting to catch on back then—but from a love of Greek mythology. It hadn't been high on Rhonda's list, but she relented in exchange for my agreeing to the name Amy Lou if it was a daughter. Yes Dad I know, you've told me many times how glad you are we weren't born female.

The newspapers call us Jason Cooper, of course. But Dad and I kept up the use of our old names with each other while we endured the long frustration of babyhood, waiting for my son's body to develop the motor skills to support intelligible speech. For the record, my name is Richard and his is Clarence. The state can believe it's gassing somebody named Jason if it wants to, but I'm telling you there never was any such person, leastways not one with an identity separate and distinct from me and my father. We suspect most reincarnates, being singletons, forget who they were and simply fall for the new identity their mom and dad foist upon them. But we, as doubles, were able to keep Richard and Clarence alive inside the putative Jason we might otherwise have become.

After word of the accident reached them, Arlene stayed on longer than she'd planned with Rhonda. The two women comforted each other in mourning our deaths, but their joy in Jason's upbringing brought his mother and grandmother even closer. Arlene eventually sold her home in Chico and moved in with Rachel. Wilma, on the other hand, was spooked by death. She gave her daughter a motherly thump on the brow, glared down at baby Jason, shuddered, crossed herself, and boarded the first plane back to the Midwest.

We're telling you all this because there's no way you can understand why we did what we did unless you know who we are and what it was like growing up this way. But for our own peace of mind, we'll spare you those details. Suffice it to say that we did not like being dictated to by the women we loved. By the time we were able to talk, we realized that no one was going to believe our story and that even if they did, some agency would take us away from Arlene and Rhonda for a lifetime of cold scrutiny. So we kept mum —and thereby kept Mom and Grandmom too, if you'll pardon our humor. Our greatest challenge was chasing away erectile manfriends, but a bit of strategic mayhem beyond our years and one or two well-calculated glances from hell kept the motherfucking to a minimum.

Our infancy and toddlerdom and childhood weren't the worst of it by any means. When puberty struck, we nearly went crazy. We'd both forgotten—given the sleep of the hairless genital in childhood—what it feels like when the hormones surge up for the first time, raging and roaring like typhoons through an adolescent body. And it was even worse for us because we understood from the outset what it all meant. As for girls our own age, our grown-up manner fascinated adults but kept our peers ever adversarial; besides which we neither of us felt much propensity toward pedophilia. So their chests

91

filled out and their thighs went soft and curvy and they got that self-conscious wary look about their tender faces, but Dad and I paid them no mind. Understand our dilemma: The women we loved we'd already married. They lived right down the hall from us, growing no younger as the clock stole away moment after moment. And our enthusiastic young cock—sprouting thick curls of brown hair all around and popping up far fatter and longer, we were pleased to note, than either of us had been in our truck-crushed, fire-whomped bodies—took to them like a compass needle takes to magnetic north.

It was touch and go for a while, learning to feel okay about jacking Jason off. I'd hidden that sort of thing from Dad, and he never talked to me about the ins and outs of lovemaking and the rest of it except when I reached ten and he muttered something about "sex rearing its ugly head" and tossed some bland vaguely Presbyterian book of cautions and platitudes in my lap. And we were father and son after all, engaging in what felt, the first couple of times, uncomfortably like homosexuality. But we made the necessary adjustments in our thinking—one always does to get what one's body craves—and relaxed into it like the old hands we were.

But ever and always, Arlene and Rhonda moved through the house, and we had to be on our guard not to be caught leering at them and not to demonstrate anything more than filial and grandfilial affection. We buried ourselves in bookishness, skipping over the stuff we recalled from our previous schooling and delving into new areas of knowledge with a depth that astounded our teachers and made us the loathed bespectacled pariah of the class of '88. With our stratospheric SAT scores and the enthusiastic support of the Hiram Johnson faculty, we wowed our way into Berkeley and began work toward a degree in 20th century history—we had, after all, lived through most of it, and current affairs had always been our strong suit.

It was in American History that we met Lorelei Meeks, she of the owl eyes and large glasses, breastless, thin as a rail, blank of face, and devoid of personality. Lorelei was a non-entity, a vacuum of need, a woman who faded into every background. Her body begged to be written upon and we, with our fat fountain-pen full of sperm, scribbled all over her. Whatever it struck our fancy to do with her she gave in to. Dad and I divvied up her holes. Every pinch of flesh was ours to caress and lubricate and shackle up and slap until it blushed or bruised or bled. And in the morning, after a shower, she'd be wiped clean again like a newly sponged chalkboard, empty as Orphan Annie's eyes and yearning to be used anew. Our grades suffered, for which we made Lorelei pay in welts and cigarette burns, and in enemas of ice-cold Coors.

At Thanksgiving we brought her home.

We thought we could divert our river of rage onto our wispy girlfriend. We thought that having a receptacle we could empty our lust into any time we liked would lessen our desire for our former spouses or at least allow us to keep it under control. But we were wrong, as wrong as a Biblethumper. We found out just how wrong when the front door swung open and our two beloved soulmates, all smiles, welcomed Jason and his dear Lorelei into the home Rhonda and I had built in the spring of '71.

While we sat in the living room, going through the maddening ritual of "introducing the girlfriend to the family," all sorts of bells and whistles were going off inside our head. My dad stole glances at Arlene, her hair gone white now, dignified lines of age making more lovely the face he hadn't caressed as a lover for nearly twenty years. She seemed genuinely spritely in her deep blue dress and her pearls, and her short white hair hugged her head just so. But I was in agony over Rhonda, looking sexier than ever at forty, stylish in her washed-out jeans and bulky breast-defining sweater. Her hair tumbled long and blond down her back, soft and springy and natural in a way that brought to mind her blond pubic softness and the sweet pink labia so long denied me. Thank God they ignored Jason, choosing instead to pour their endearments into the smiling nullity that sat, legs crossed, nervously beside him on the couch.

But inside us, an idea was gathering bits of itself together. The location of rope and tools in the garage, of clean dust rags in the closet, of scissors and carving knives in the kitchen, suddenly took on grave importance. It was as if the house itself was shoving Dad and me into some inevitable sequence of bloody dance steps.

We heard Jason's thin voice fielding inane questions. From the way they received his answers, it seemed that our facade of calm was somehow being maintained. And when we moved into the dining room, watching the maddening thighs of our proper wives sway this way and that, we heard Jason announce that he had a special surprise for his three most favorite women in the world. You'd think the odds against one man subduing three women would be pretty high. And in most cases you'd be right. But people become surprisingly compliant when they're in a festive mood and someone they trust—a son or grandson for example—sets down the rules of playful bondage they must submit to in order to receive an unexpected gift. In no time they were blindfolded with their hands tied tight behind them, a predicament our dear Lorelei was used to.

Not so Arlene and Rhonda. They complained, playfully at first, then more vociferously, about the chafing of the ropes. But their protests really began in earnest when we tied their ankles to the chair legs—right to right, left to left—and removed their shoes. People tend to be funny that way about their feet.

We let them sit there complaining into unresponsive air while we lowered the blinds and gathered tools. Some of the things our hands lifted off the garage pegboard or dug out of the drawers in the kitchen astonished us at the time, made us worry we'd gone off the deep end, though on hindsight they all made perfect sense. Once we had them laid out on the rug, our first order of business was the unclothing of our women. Because garments are not easily stripped from bound limbs, we used Rhonda's pinking shears for most of it. Arlene freaked when we scissored away her stockings, maybe from the feel of the cold metal moving up along her thighs, I can't be sure. Her shrieks spiked out into these absurd high-pitched bursts that sounded like a jackal in a trap. So hard were they

94

on the ears that we decided to remove her blindfold and gag her with it. We did our best to ignore the look in her eyes; it was too painful to dwell on for any length of time. Dad was a little bit ashamed of her, weren't you Dad? I mean at that point we hadn't so much as broken skin, we hadn't even hinted that that's where things were headed, yet already Arlene was huffing and going all red in the face like McMurphy being electroshocked in *Cuckoo's Nest*.

Rhonda was a lot cooler about things, asking her son what he was doing, keeping her voice as calm and soothing as she could. When we felt like answering her, which was seldom, we kept our responses brief and noncommittal. We preferred letting our Fiskars do the talking for us. We liked their unrelenting ways, the steady rise and fall of the alligator mouth, the steel bite of perfectly zigzagged teeth, the falling away of fabric, and the slow, hypnotic unveiling of forbidden flesh. From the look of Rhonda's private parts, a bit puffy and vaguely gleaming, we half suspected our perversity was turning her on.

You can imagine the effect all this snipping away of blouses and bras and panties was having on us. But mixed in with the arousal was a sadness, a bitter sorrow at the ravages of time on human flesh. Here, emerging one sharp snip at a time, were the beloved bodies of our dear wives, hidden away for nearly twenty years. Our idle fantasies at childhood's end, our torrid love affair with onanism in adolescence, our imagined substitutions of these two women when we squeezed shut our eyes and eased into Lorelei—all of that had been erected on memories two decades old. We were ill-prepared to witness the accumulated assaults of age on their flesh: the sag, the flab, the withdrawal of vibrancy and resilience and muscle tone.

We dimmed the lights.

When we finished denuding our women, we took Rhonda's suggestion and turned up the thermostat. I was able to convince Dad, despite his initial resistance, that we too ought to disrobe. His preference was to unzip, reach into our shorts, and bring out into the open Jason's erection only; but I argued that we were, after all, going to be doing more than simply fucking the odd vagina and that it would be far easier to shower blood off our skin than to remove it from our best suit, and he, inordinately fond of that suit (his taste, not mine), could only agree. So we removed Rhonda's and Lorelei's blindfolds, not wanting to limit our display to Arlene only, and slow-stripped for our three naked mates. It's fair to say we surprised ourselves—Wouldn't you agree, Dad?—with our prowess as ecdysiasts. I sincerely believe we turned the ladies on, even Arlene gasping behind her gag; I can testify that we surely turned ourselves on.

Not to put too fine a point on it, we pleasured them, our wives and the vapidity they flanked. If they played at resistance, which one or two of them did, we read their coyness as a come on, and came on. At one point, Rhonda, acting the castrating bitch, snapped at our penis, but we had matters well in hand and snatched it free of her cruel jaws, backhanding her for her naughtiness and clamping our own choppers on her left nipple until she screamed out an apology profuse enough to satisfy us. Even so, we steered clear of her mouth thereafter, though memories of my lusty young spouse feasting at my groin during our married life drew me back to her lips again and again, and Dad had to intervene several times for the sake of our manhood.

Finally, when we'd gotten as close to our women as we were going to get without breaking skin, Dad and I began our failed—albeit noble—experiment. Looking back, it astounds us that we never once questioned the fundamental wisdom of what we were doing. But in this short, sorry life, one moment often leads to the next without time to entertain consequences. There seemed an inevitability in operation at the time, a passionate surging forth which no attempt at mere reason stood a chance against. Maybe all of our synapses weren't firing properly that day, or maybe something inside of us snapped. Whatever the reason, we forged ahead.

From the way Arlene and Rhonda were behaving, it was clear they would never consent to the group marriage idea that had occurred to us first. The very gathering of the tools— the saws, the screwdrivers, the staple gun—was surely our subliminal recognition that that scenario was not about to play itself out. To our unsettled minds, that left but one option: the scavenging of our wives' bodies and the bold reconstitution of what we liberated from those hallowed grounds into as near perfection as we could get on the blank canvas of Lorelei's body.

We began with the teeth. To our surprise, Lorelei resisted. But a small clamp at either corner of her jaws rendered her struggles pointless. Although our first extractions were bumbling and amateurish, before long we were uprooting her stubborn molars with all the élan of any D.D.S. out there. When only gums remained, we found some cotton balls in the medicine cabinet to plug our ears with. Lorelei's gurgled screams were no joy to listen to, and we suspected that Arlene and Rhonda, once we began on them, would be no less merciless in their protests.

I hated what came next. Each of us, as you might imagine, was partial to his own wife's dentition, so we decided, after heated debate, to alternate extractions, taking the odd-numbered teeth from Arlene and the evens from Rhonda. To keep them in their proper sequence, and to counter our worries that teeth, like seedlings, might require immediate transplant to remain viable, we followed each tooth's removal with its immediate insertion into Lorelei's gums, tapping them in as gently as possible so as not to injure their roots. What I hated about all of this were the heartrending screams of my wife and mother. I wasn't prepared for the way their distant cries tore through my innards, making my brain beat with pain.

It grew worse when we began on the fingernails. Dad cursed me for a coward but I hung back and let him perform the slicing, and pliering, and supergluing on his own. I felt bruised and blistered everywhere inside.

Still shaken, I joined Dad in shaving Lorelei's head, removing her ears, and stitching Arlene's on. But when it came time to scalp my dear sweet Rhonda, I couldn't bring myself—in spite of my lust for her lovely blond hair—to help him grasp and guide the X-Acto knife and the scraping tools. Instead, I tried, over the static of my father's anger, to soothe

Rhonda's torments. I assured her, though I'd begun to doubt it myself, that once she left her own body and moved into Lorelei's with Arlene, she'd come to appreciate the diligence with which we had harvested her hair and understand that the agonies we were putting her through were worth the final result. She did nothing but scream bloody murder and strain her abraded limbs against her bonds.

I wept openly then, while Dad bent, grim-faced, to his bloody task and pressed the blond skullcap down onto Lorelei's bare, glue-smeared scalp.

Next came the mammaries. There was little point in giving our lovely new bride long tumbling blond tresses if what they tumbled down onto was a couple of flat nubs rather than the breathtaking swell of two hefty kissable lickable squeezable suckable breasts. Dad and I were used to that kind of pleasure, given the endowments of our old wives. But we found ourselves once again at loggerheads, and it was worse now because Dad had by this time lost all patience with me. Rhonda and Arlene both sported superb knockers and we were not about to break up a set by taking one from each woman. Yet Lorelei barely had room on her chest for two decent-sized tits, let alone four. In the end we decided to fasten one pair to her front and another to her back. I lost the coin toss, but I don't think it's sour grapes to say that I got the better of the bargain, because our first mastectomy came off rather badly and in my opinion—You just keep still, Dad!—in my opinion, we botched Arlene's breasts badly. When it came to Rhonda, who was pleading like a little girl at this point, I was ready to refuse the carving knife again, but Dad jammed an awl into my left arm. Then he gave me a powerful talking to, really chewing me out good—"The next time it's your balls, boy!", that sort of thing. I know you meant it, Dad; just shut your yap. Anyway, partly because of what Dad said and partly because I wanted the job done right, I helped with the second operation, which I believe we carried out with a greater sense of professionalism and pride. What did I care about having to go behind our new woman's back to get to Rhonda's breasts as long as they retained their full loveliness?

We were in the midst of the arduous task of making a vulval triptych across Lorelei's stretched inner thighs, parenthesizing Lorelei's pussy with the harvested quims of our wives, when there came a distant pounding at the door, and a trio of faces filling one windowpane briefly with ugliness, and then a loud intrusive sound like crunching wood. One pair of arms grabbed us from behind and another handcuffed us, and the rest of the night was nothing but sirens and naked rides and cold baths and damp blankets and question after question after question. You know the rest. Aside from discounting our reincarnation story and sensationalizing out of all proportion what we did, the Bee and the Union did a fair job of reporting the truth.

What did we learn from all this?

We learned that happiness can't be forced. It's not something that yields to a desperate scheme and a crosscut saw. It's not something you can construct. We tried to piece it together bit by bit and we failed. Those of you out there whose minds may be starting to warp the same way ours did, take my advice and forget it. If kind words and gentle persuasion don't get you what you want, then cheese graters and electric drills and large knives with serrated edges aren't going to do it either. We tried. We failed. And we're going to pay for it. Next time, whoever's body we end up in, we're not even going to think about doing anything like this again.

At least I won't.

Dad tells me he's planning to major in pre-med.

THE SLOBBERING TONGUE THAT ATE THE FRIGHTFULLY HUGE WOMAN

Sally Holmes was married to a swell guy. She liked working in the lab. Holding clipboards and making notes for Doctor Baxter while hiding her beauty behind glasses and a tight bun was her idea of fun. She did it well.

And she gave her husband John a nice home. Soon, if they could figure out where children came from, there'd be pattering feet to feed. John was a good man. They'd been childhood sweethearts. Now John was a police lieutenant. She didn't understand his work. Heck, truth be told, she barely understood her own. But all Sally had to do was to poise her fountain pen smartly above her clipboard and act as if she were saying clever things, and Doctor Baxter was more than pleased to keep her around.

The one thing Sally liked about Doctor Baxter, other than her paycheck, was his way with words. He was a blob in pretty much every respect, balding, sags of flesh stuck on his face like sneezed boogers on a mirror. But when he spoke, his labials, his fricatives, his palatals, his urps of intelligence, the way his moist pink tongue oystered in his mouth—all of those oral sorts of things made Sally go all soft and squoozy inside.

For months he'd been working on something top secret, putting in so many hours he might as well have camped out at the institute. He let no one into his inner lab. But the notes he dictated tantalized her. He overworked his staff, but Sally didn't mind (she knew that *John* did). It just meant more toward their nest egg, more smart repartee over the clipboard, and more of that clever tongue.

When Doctor Baxter invited her that evening into his inner lab, just him and her around, Sally had no inkling that anything more than science was on his mind. He held the unsealed door for her, and she stepped in, sniffing a barnyard stench she'd caught wind of before.

John lay there in his pajamas, wanting his wife next to him. It felt so great to hug her, pajamas to pajamas, and give her a pristine little kiss goodnight. And every so often—once every few months if he was lucky—she'd be open to cuddling in the dark, to undoing certain strategic snaps and letting him shoot an icky mess inside her while she lay there so calm and sweet and receptive. He'd give his standard "Sorry" in her ear, then roll off her, shame in him yes, but feeling glad too that she hid her disgust so well.

It proved she loved him.

Still, he sensed there was something missing in their marriage. As Sally flitted about the kitchen or Hoovered the rugs or knelt to dust the baseboards, John felt as if there were a crack in her smile—almost as if, God forbid, a first wrinkle were appearing in that smooth peach-infant face of hers.

His wife needed reassurance.

Oh, heck. He'd drop in at the lab. Yes, yes. He'd dare to be different. Flinging the covers back, he leaped out of bed. Would he put on the clothing he'd tossed into the hamper? No. New ones. He wouldn't sweat too much in them and he could wear them again tomorrow.

Sally'd be thrilled to see him. A sweet surprise.

Baxter anticipated her amazement.

"Oh, my!" she ejaculated, her fetching shoulderblades flexing like coy airplane struts under that white coat she plumped out so well in front.

"You've never seen a ten-foot cock before?" The bird was indeed awesome there in its cage, its magnificent head turned in quirk, one squint-eye wide as a saucer. Too bad he hadn't chosen a hen for his experiments. She would've made one heck of a meal, and there were other interesting avenues (so to speak) that might have been explored. He was tired of cleaning up after Giganto here, and tired of feeding him. Damn rooster was due for death.

"Goodness, Doctor Baxter," Sally exclaimed. "What've you been up to?"

"See that?" he said, pointing to the bell jar on the table, with its throbbing pink crystal. "I concocted that substance. I call it gargantuum. It makes organic matter grow. Don't ever disturb that glass container, or there's no telling what will happen."

"I won't." She shook her pretty little head so that her radiant tresses primped and fluffed like in a shampoo commercial; no, wait, he was imagining that. Her bun held her hair tight, severe, puckered like a clenched rectum.

Baxter stepped in front of her. "But that's not why I invited you into my inner lab."

"It isn't?"

"No." He eased the carving knife from his cavernous coat pocket. "I'd like you to undress for me, Sally—nice and slow, nice and sexy, one button, one snap at a time."

Sally blanched fetchingly. "I can't do that."

He placed the blade against her neck. "You can," he insisted, "and you will. But first, undo that god-awful, fershlugginer bun. Let your Prellity down, sweetcakes."

Tears welled up as she reached to free her hair. Her breasts rose with the motion. Doctor Baxter fixed on them with those ugly eyes of his. He was a loathsome lunk of a man. Except for his tongue. Poor thing seemed shanghai'd into saying awful things, but somehow that didn't diminish its beauty.

The magnitude of her anger startled her.

Sally'd never been angry about anything in her life, not one blessed thing.

But, even as her fingers worked the buttons and tears gathered in her eyes, she was angry about this. Her anger was hot and solid, coming deep from her insides but hiding itself as it grew. He couldn't detect it. But she could surely feel it.

And soon, but she feared not soon enough, it would lash out at the scientist Sally had trusted to be good but who was very bad indeed.

"Not fast enough," he said. His free hand shot forth and yanked her lapel to one side, so that her white satin slip showed from her right shoulder strap down to where it cupped in lacy fullness her huge right breast. Where his brutish paw touched her, her flesh ached.

She looked at the knife in his hand, the sharp blade, the brown rippled wood of its handle. She wanted so badly to wrest it away from him, to use it on him.

"Faster!" he said, drool dripping from his lips. You never knew about people. You just never knew.

John adored being a police lieutenant. All the boys in blue, nice decent Christian fellas, loved and respected you. You got to wear stylish suits with papercut creases ironed into the legs. They snugged your badge into a real nice soft-leather case that felt as cozy as suede when you whipped it from your inside coat pocket and held it up for a citizen's eyes.

He maneuvered the Plymouth along the quiet streets, a bouquet of long-stemmed roses lying beside him.

A lanky young man was walking an Airedale. John hit his horn lightly, waved, took the return wave. The dog's no-nonsense yap filled the air with glee. Life was good. Life was very good. Life was very very very good.

But it could be better.

He could assure Sally that he loved her, that there'd never be for him any woman in the world but her. That was what a wife wanted to hear. For John, there'd only always been Sally. No one else. And there never *would* be anyone else. Never never never.

He hummed a sprightly tune.

There was Baxter Enterprises ahead. The guard at the gate grinned at him. He lifted the flowers, said, "For my sweet honey," and the mustachioed geezer in uniform nodded and waved him through. "Say hello to the missus for me," the guard shouted, shrinking in the rear view mirror.

103

"I will," yelled John. He rolled up the window, the corners of his mouth hurting from his smiles, and pressed on toward the main building.

Baxter had his way with her. Though smart and snappy as always, Miss Holmes was passive like a good dolly ought to be. On the floor, upon the air mattress he forced her into blowing up, he felt all her secret places, he tasted her, he lay his bulky frame on her and forced his manhood inside her. The air was thick with bird smell, tainted by hints of formaldehyde from the embryos jarred on the table above them.

So enthralled did he become and so passive and almost not-there was his victim that he lost track of his carving knife. And suddenly there was a tugging at his hand, and an emptiness there. Then his shoulder caught fire, a jag of outrage sinking thickly inside. His secretary wiggled like a ba-zillion panicked eels out from under him as the pain erupted, a swift deep cramp in his upper torso.

He screamed, not continuous but blips—sharp, barked, like a wounded mutt. Her face flared and bloomed. Shrew, he thought. Termagant. That's what she had turned into. She gripped the knife handle and yanked it out. He felt somehow as if his lungs followed it, and yet it was a hurt he needed from her. She had repented. She would help him to a hospital, stanch his blood, bandage him, make him all better, hold him, kiss him, dump her dorky boy in blue.

Then she docked him. She fisted his shaft, razored a chill below, pressed it in, cutting through no-resistance, through sponge cake, burrowing and spreading a volcano of agony. Her first thrust had enervated him. He could only make faint shows of protest as she unmanned him. Suddenly he could no longer feel the squeeze, although he saw the purple flesh blanch in her fingers, saw her pry his member away, felt his groin skin peel up, a gigantic splinter of pain, toward his navel.

His thing thwapped on the floor where she tossed it.

He rocked and screamed, energy draining from between his legs. His attacker—*he'd* been the attacker; now *she* was—bounded up, clattered in his tools above, came back with a bone saw.

And then, oh my god, she severed his hands.

***

Rage drove her on. This monster had touched her in all her secret places. Now she was dismantling him, all his offending parts off and away. That's the way it had to be, Sally's crazed mind told her.

His resistance was all in his voice. The bone saw snagged on the air mattress, which burbled its air away through washes of blood. But the vile hand snapped off, cracking and tearing like an uncooked lobsterclaw. The other, as his stump feebly brushed her back with sticky protest, proved even easier.

Time for his tongue.

She'd brought back a bull castrator—why he had one, she didn't stop to ask. But her bloody hands tore at his jaws and jammed the instrument deep down into his throat, watching the tongue slither in snug where a pizzle would ordinarily go. Then she clamped shut, freshets of blood upshooting, spraying her breasts with hot gore. And out the quivering tantalizing tormenting sucker came.

Though it too had violated her, she didn't toss the tongue to the floor as she'd done with his hands and his manhood. She rose, unlidded the first jar she saw, took out the chick embryo, and dropped in the tongue, lifting the jar, hugging its chill to her breasts.

She was aimlessly meandering, slowly, randomly, her face a veil of tears, wounded tears, tears of rage.

Sally's foot struck something. She glanced down at it, Baxter's right hand. The things it had done! Still with the jar hugged to her chest, she bent down, snatched the odious thing up and hurled it away from her.

The bell jar rang from the impact, lifted, tottered, and fell with a decisive clatter to the tabletop, rolling off and shattering on the floor. The pink crystal pulsed and hummed. Its light filled the air. The sound it made rose, higher, higher, like a menacing theremin.

And then the explosion came, pink goop in the air, on her flesh, down her throat. It coated her arms where they hugged the jar, radiating there, pulsing. Sally wanted to scream, but she choked on the stuff, and felt it strangely warm all over her.

***

Just as John killed the Plymouth, he felt a *whumph* in the air. It was a subtle pop but all his antennas of love and protection immediately sprang up and out.

Sally was in danger.

Without remembering how he'd done it, he was suddenly outside the car, his hands on the closed pinging car door. It felt as if it took forever but he raced to the entrance and plowed through, down corridor upon corridor to Sally's lab. "Sally!" he yelled. "Sally! Sally! Sally!"

No one.

But John took in the door to the inner lab, its edge blasted and pulsing pink from lights within. He dashed to it, yanked it open.

His wife was facing away from him, naked and sobbing.

On the floor lay Doctor Baxter, parts of him missing, him nearly dead but not quite so. A gigantic rooster stood in a cage in the far corner, stinking the place up.

John approached his naked wife. There was yucky pink stuff in her hair, all over her body, on the jar her hands gripped so tight. The residue of some pink substance lay like shards of shattered icicle on a far table.

"Honey?" he said. "Are you okay?"

Her face was slabbed in tears.

She looked down, noticed what she was holding, set it with other jars like it on the table beside her.

She turned to him, held out her hands but then raised them as he approached. "I . . . I'm all goopy."

"Here." He looked around wildly, saw some linen on a shelf. "I'll get you a towel."

He got her a towel.

Doctor Baxter, gurgling, died. "He attacked me," she said. John nodded. His wife was one savage biddy. But, by God, she'd had good reason. There was cleanup needing to be done, here and in their lives. But he vowed, by his love for her, to see things through to the end.

***

Baxter woofed his last breath. His mouth, his groin, his wriststumps felt as if God, frowning from on high, had snapped bear traps on them and salted his wounds, skewering his celestial disapproval in like sharp smoldering stakes that glowed white hot, turning, twisting, searing, never a dull moment in his tormented body.

Then suddenly the pain, pricklike, was cut off.

He was somewhere else. Somewhere cool and moist and cloying. He couldn't see. He couldn't hear. But he felt himself alive and whole, if uprooted. And he could taste, oh yes he could. Yucky tasting stuff; unpalatable, though he had no palate.

But something most succulent lay close by, something he had tasted recently and could still, in sensual memory, recall with wicked delight. He pulsed. He surged. But this new body, if that's what it was—limbless, but mere limb—would take some getting used to, to make it motile, to seek out and taste that recalled succulence once more.

A light shone, warm and pink (now how could he sense, being blind, colors?), a finger's reach from him. It felt like sunlight on seedlings. He sensed arousal, the shift of flexible flesh, an overpowering urge to grow.

In bed that night, after the police procedurals had swept through her, Sally tossed and turned. An extra long bath had helped, steaming there, quite out of it, till the water grew cool. But she still felt Doctor Baxter's vile acts clinging to her— that and the glowing pink goop, the gargantuum the explosion had drenched her with.

At midnight, she woke in a sweat.

John was snoring beside her, big long snuffly snorts that made him less than appealing. His exhalations stank like sodden cigars, like burnt toast threaded with maggoty shreds of pork.

When Sally shifted to turn him on his side, away from her, her pajamas clung tight. The buttons strained at her breasts, alternating left-and-right-facing vees of fabric. Her hips drew the cloth taut as snapped sheets. Breathing was difficult. Had she put on a pair of John's pajamas by mistake? Nope. The monogram, a red SAH, was hers.

John snorted awake.

"You okay?" he mumbled.

"Yes," she said. "Go back to sleep."

She tried to do the same. Funny. Her pajama bottoms used to cover her ankles. Now they'd started to creep up her calves, clinging there like wet wraps of seaweed.

She dismissed it, tried to find sleep. But Baxter's words of warning and the image of a ten-foot cock refused to leave her mind.

John feigned sleep. But it wouldn't come. In the moonlight seeping in their window, he let his glistening eyes open. His wife lay upon her back, dozing fitfully. It was a warm night. The covers slanted at her waist.

My God, he thought, her breasts are mammoth.

Sally was so beautiful. It tore him up inside that she'd endured the nightmare of being violated by Doctor Baxter. The warped deviant deserved to have his . . . but then John remembered. Baxter *had* had his . . . And by Sally's dear hand.

He propped himself slowly on one crooked arm, head in hand, and beheld her. Sweet face. Wanton hair, down now, rioting like rainbows on her pillow. Somehow, there seemed *more* of her tonight. He loved her so. He wished there were some way he could undo her pain.

Undo her buttons.

Her breasts were so huge. Pregnant women, he'd been told, got that way. Maybe they'd have a child after all. But he doubted that. They plumped there under the strain of cotton, huge soft cantaloupe mounds that would one day droop and sag like ugly sacks of pudding, but didn't now. They cantilevered, as magic as flying buttresses in their firmness, their heft, their suspension.

One day, maybe, Sally would let him see them naked.

But that day, he knew, lay far in the future. His wife was

no slut. And she'd been through a personal hell that would take time and patience to heal.

The bastard (oops, he amended it to "bad man") ought to have his . . .

Ah yes. Small favors.

Baxter felt in-tight. Jar-shaped. He had to get out before the confinement squeezed him to death. He'd never felt so helpless. Then he realized, with a virtual smack to his nonexistent forehead, that he was all muscle.

He contracted, tensed. Waited until he felt cramped again. Then, abruptly, he flexed.

And suddenly he was free!

Sensing sharpness, he gingerly moved over fragments so as not to cut himself. He tasted wood, fell, thwapped to newly mopped linoleum tile. Licking the ammoniac tang of Mr. Clean, he pulsed and throbbed toward freedom.

A pressure halted him. He smelled the black stink of Cat's Paw shoe polish. Swooping across leather, he found flesh, flesh that shook, jittered. Panicked hands batted at him. But he clung tight, wrapping about an ankle. His spittle turned the flesh soft and absorbable. He took the stuff in, the blood, the bone, lapping up thigh meat as his victim fell, scream-vibes egging him on.

It felt positively erotic to sate himself.

Like lava, he smacked up the body inside the clothes, tasted groin slit, hair, belly, breasts. A female cop, was his guess as he gobbled. And alone, based on the help she didn't get. His tonguebody thinned and imbibed, slapping like a wave, receding, drawing sandflesh, sandbone, after it, trails of bloodbubble foaming behind.

When nothing remained but copsuit, he ambled on.

Sally, by the dresser, held her glasses confusedly in her hand. The arms had snapped when she tried to put them on. But strangely she could see fine without them.

"Listen," John said to her. "I'll take the day off. I've got time. We'll go to the beach."

"You think that would help?" Nothing would help.

"It's worth a try."

After a time, she relented. Her husband seemed to be standing in a hole, but he was solid and assuring. It was a blessing to be in his care. When she took her one-piece into the bathroom to change, it wouldn't fit.

So they got in the car and went to Macy's.

For some reason a white bikini, one of those new and daring suits, seemed right. When she looked at herself in the dressing room mirror, Anita Ekberg came to mind. Milk bottles. My, my, she thought, I *am* filling out.

She could scarcely pull her clothing over it, the red checked shirt, the slacks. Was it time to diet? No. She wasn't fatter. Just larger. Hmmm.

"Let's go," she said, taking John's arm.

On the drive to the beach, she brooded on gargantuum.

Jones Beach was crowded that day. Must be lots of folks on vacation, John thought. They strolled along the shore, his wife's statuesque body—and since when had she become statuesque?—drawing stares. There was no hope of finding seclusion, but between beachfronts, they found a bit more room to spread out the pea-green army blanket.

At a distance, an unchaperoned bunch of teens played jungle music, tinny, from a tiny transistor radio.

Sally tucked her hair into a bathing cap, white with plastic flowers daisied on it. John frolicked with her in the waves, splashing her, being splashed. For the moment, everything seemed normal again.

Back on the blanket, her body glistened with droplets as she lay down. Sleek curvy back. Wondrous front. What a full voluptuous woman his wife was. Odd. In the store, her bikini had fit fine. Now the flesh strained at it and he fancied he could see the cloth tugging, thinning.

"Jeepers, this suit is tight," she said.

John looked over at the teens. They were jiggling to the radio noise. Disgusting. America was in trouble.

He heard Sally prepare a sneeze.

When he turned to her, the sneeze blew into her hand and her suit exploded off her. For a second in the bright sunlight, his wife was bare-ass naked.

She took the Lord's name in vain.

Then she grabbed a towel, two towels, and sat there rocking, crying, lamenting, "What's *happening* to me?"

Baxter tasted dirt, gravel, cinders, dog doo, hawked gobs of spit. He preferred the lady cop. He craved more female flesh, and one dainty dish in particular. When he picked up the tracks of his former secretary, he'd be hot on that cutie's trail, no question.

But in the meantime, he slithered along the edge of downtown North Allville. Somehow his senses of taste and touch were so acute, he could grope along an internal map of the town. He had ghost visions, ghost hearings, faint white whispered things, that corresponded to what was out there.

A malt shop near the railroad tracks.

He sniffed females, lots of them.

The air jittered with passion sounds. He could feel the floor shaking as he slid through the open door. There were seven of them, smelling like high school cheerleader types. With his tip, he eased the door closed, locked it, turned the OPEN sign to CLOSED.

High giggles knifed the air.

Ponytails twirled, hips gyred in long poodle skirts.

Then he attacked, and the giggles turned to screams.

He sucked up girlflesh, swelled, grew. This was the life. Blood, bone, bile, chocolate malts half-digested in smooth taut burst tummies.

Much better than dog doo.

But nowhere near as delectable as sweet Sally Holmes.

Weeks passed. The evidence of Sally's transformation had become so clear that, the day after the beach fiasco, she fled. Nearly seven feet. She was growing and growing fast. As she left, she had to duck through the front door to avoid braining herself.

111

She kept to the woods during the day, moving at night in a direction that called to her. To clothe herself, she stole sheets off lines, pinning them together with wooden clothespins. She raided gardens, wishing she had money to pay the good people she stole from.

Her mind was expanding too. Her rage. And, God help her, her libido. She'd never been so horny and so angry, and her thoughts had never ranged so widely over being and nothingness, the meaning of life, and the silly putterings of the diminutive creatures she espied from where she hid. Whole passages of Plato and Aristotle she had slid over in school now came back, making sense. She embraced what was right in them, tossed what was wrong.

When she was thirty feet tall, she began not to care who saw her move at night. At forty feet, she bared her breasts, feeling nightbreeze and sunlight tauten the huge nipples. At fifty feet, she started to tease the little people, gripping cars and jiggling them, lifting them by the roofs so swiftly that sometimes—like painfully inept special effects—it seemed she lifted the landscape along with it. She wrecked upright structures. Steeples, radio towers, anything lofty she tore off, feeling enraged and good and sweaty. During the day, she sought out bowllike depressions, cool, lush, comforting, to sleep in.

She had no idea what place instinct drew her toward, but it was good, very good indeed. Of that she was sure.

John fixed upon the US map the sergeant was pointing to. The country was going crazy. His wife, breasts bare as a harlot's, had grown huge and was destroying property left and right. Rumors of a giant tongue circulated, and whole villages' populations disappearing. The only thing left behind? A trail of bloody saliva.

"Mrs. Holmes was spotted here (*thwap*), here (*thwap*), and here (big *thwap*)," the man said. He was square-jawed and steely-eyed. "You men notice where she's headed?"

Everyone grumbled a yes like they were in church with their heads bowed muttering amen.

"That's right," he said. "The Grand Canyon. We can let her be, then zoom in with helicopters, pick her off."

"Hold on," said John. "That's my wife you're talking about."

"Don't be a chump for love," said the sergeant. "We have a public nuisance on our hands. And I aim to wash it off. With steel slugs of civic soap."

"Have you no heart, man?"

"I have a duty to all Americans. That, über alles."

Everyone grumbled yeah, yeah.

John grabbed the pointer. "Listen, men, I know Sally as well as anyone. I can reason with her, persuade her to stop destroying erect edifices."

"She's a monster!"

"She's my *wife*!!!!!"

He put it so strongly, the other cops relented.

The sergeant rested a hand on John's shoulder. John knew he wasn't a bad man. Just a jerk.

"Time to get *you* to the Grand Canyon," he said.

And it was.

Baxter loomed at the edges of the drive-in. The film splashed up there, from his honed sensors, he supposed was some dark and scary thing. Good. Made it easier for him to claim victims. Black night, black screen, black cover.

He liked the juicy females, the ones the crewcut boys liquefied with their fingers, squirming out of clothing as easily as out of their virginity.

In the back row a Dodge rocked. He could tell it was a Dodge because his tip traced the chrome letters. Baxter tasted unwashed car, skimmed through the window crack, and dove for the couple in the back seat. He hated boy-taste, but (just as he'd saved the best for last over dinner as a boy) he absorbed the boyfriend first, while he muffled the screams of the half-dressed dolly. Then he turned his all to savoring dessert.

She was mere appetizer, a speared shrimp.

Sally Holmes' sweetness lay on the wind, and Baxter's drool slathered his pathway toward her. In his future, he sensed a deep wide all-engulfing hole.

***

Sally recognized it of course. She and John on their honeymoon had spent time here, had gone down on donkeys.

The Grand Canyon.

Then it had felt like love.

Now it felt like home.

Oblivious to the gaping miniatures scurrying about at her feet, she unpinned the diaperlike loincloth whose taut clutch vexed her, dropped it, and started her long descent to the bottom where the river was.

One weird-eyed maniac feasted his eyes on her, as she lowered her nude body over the rim. She jiggled her boobs at him, then took a deep breath and blew him, midst debris and rubble, back toward the panicked masses. Lustily, she laughed. Then the rim rose above her skull and she was on her way, night's gravid moon lighting rock and brush along the trail.

The local police tracked her with binoculars and with telescopes, relaying her whereabouts to John at the lowest point of the canyon.

When he came upon her, she was reclining, buck naked, near the river. She was obscene. She was beautiful. His shame, under his pants, grew hard. His wife's hand was on her womanhood, stirring it like she stirred cake batter in her Betty Crocker apron. Her deep throaty moans echoed in the vast rocky gorge.

"Sally," he shouted. She didn't hear him. He yelled her name over and over until he grew hoarse.

Then she noticed him. A look of desire burned in her eyes. "John," she intoned, a deep throbbing need there.

"My dear darling," he mourned, "they say there may be an antidote, they say—"

She grabbed him, not hard, but firm as one might grab a kitten or gerbil. "Fuck antidotes," she said in rumbles of husky thunder. "I *like* being big."

He chided her for her crude language, but she merely

laughed, booming, like the genie in *The Thief of Baghdad*.
Then she brought him within whiffing distance of her womanhood. He recognized the morning-after manhood stink (but writ large and overpowering) before his bath.

"Make like a statue," she ordered. "Rigidify."

Before he could ask her why, he found *out* why.

Like a diver just before splitting the silent water, he took a breath. That saved him. Into warm gooshy hugs of pudding he was thrust, splooshing about in smooth dark pulsings that brought cows' udders to mind. It was divine and it was terrifying. Just when he knew his lungs would burst, Sally unencunted him, frotting his forehead against a ruddy nub (what *was* that thing?), above which curled riots of coarse straw abruptly thatched. Then—and by the grace of God he could sense when, so he could gulp a goopy breath—she'd plunge him back inside her, twisting him and turning him like an agitator in a washing machine, like an orange half being brutally juiced.

But abruptly he was out, laid on the ground, chilling in the night air. He blinked his stuck eyelids open. And saw— oh God he wanted to shit—a gigantic tongue throbbing not six feet away, bloated, bloody, spilling icky rivulets of drool down its unclean sides.

Baxter cared not a lick for the jerk. He'd served as—what did whores call it?—a *dildo* for Baxter's bitch.

But now the bitch had Baxter to satisfy her.

And satisfy her he would.

Tasting more sandstone powder as he rolled on, Baxter leaned against her massive thigh, slurped at her perineum, caught her spillage where it dripped, slowly slalomed his tip up the swollen slit of her excitation toward her sweet hillock of delight.

But she seized him, shoved him in. She embraced him like any animal, and he embraced the opportunity to thrust as deep as he could, elongating, conforming himself to her inner shape, vibrating, throbbing, shuddering, as he moved inward. A tiny bit of him, where she had disembodied him, jazzed at her womanhood.

But the rest was inside, not yet releasing his devouring fluid. Time enough, in orgasm, to make her die. He filled her, pulsating against her walls, sweeping beyond the cervix into the uterus itself, filling it like a plum-passioned fetus, poised to wail in ecstasy like a sweaty trumpeter nailing a string of high notes.

She was coming.

And, oh god, she was *squeezing.*

He flexed, but it did no good. She was crushing him. He tried to release the killing fluid. Got some out, felt the beginnings of meld.

But it was too tight. Too fugging tight.

Trapped.

He fluttered.

He died.

Sally tightened in orgasm. Boulders shook loose at her screams. Her husband, with his hands up to his ears, looked like a drooled-upon letter T.

But the golden tongue she'd had to have was releasing venom, was stuck inside, even as she shuddered in ecstasy. It stung her center. She felt the life squeezed off there first, even as her final orgasm played out. The hurt bled outward from her womb, attacking kidneys, pancreas, islets of Lagerhans, on and on.

Lights winked out all over her body.

"I'm dying," she gasped.

"Oh no," said the pipsqueak. "Honey, that can't be."

She tried to expel the inert tongue like unfertilized tissue, tried to yank it out. No go. It stuck there like a wasp's barb, sinking its killing force deeper with every breath.

Her lungs felt the slash of cut glass. Her heart.

"Goodbye, John," she gasped.

"I'll never forget you," he screamed. "Nobody will."

The thing that had killed her pooched out of her like a melting strawberry popsicle, dripping crimson gush along her buttocks and onto the earth. It looked like a wilted poinsettia clasped in a clutching infant's hand.

At the height of the terrible display, she had glowed pink: the same pink as in the lab that fateful day. John had felt a warmth beyond embarrassment along his front but mostly in his manhood.

"Bury me deep." Sally's eyes grew fuzzy.

John did a hasty calculation. "I'll bury you *well*," he said. He was hard. To his astonishment he didn't feel any shame. Not only was he hard. He was thick and long, much longer, much thicker than ever in his life. He felt the blunt bludgeon through his trousers. A fucking spade handle stood there.

Crude language had suddenly become okay. In fact it was a decided turn-on. His bulb-head throbbed.

Thoughts of conjunction soared in his head. Thoughts of people watching him score with lots of chicks, sticking his tool in places it had never dreamt of going before.

"Kiss me, John."

He approached her lips, thinking to peck them. Then she inhaled suddenly and he was a hotdog snug in two soggy bun-halves. But a moment later, her death, huge and final and thick with shadows, flooded out upon a slow exhalation and he fell, body-kissed, cock-kissed, to the earth.

Still erect, he picked himself up.

Sally had left him memories.

He patted his pants.

And she'd left him *this*.

And *this* would guide him henceforth on his solitary way.

HOLY FAST,
HOLY FEAST

The Voice: And what is the greatest wonder?
Yudhishthira: Day by day, hour by hour, death strikes,
and yet we live as though we will never die. That is the
greatest wonder.
  —*The Mahabharata*

Baby Jenny's last breath was a quiet one. Sealed in her space-heated radiatored bedroom, wrapped and swaddled inside a pale-yellow bassinet, the three-month old preemie lay buried beneath a miasma of ammonia. Bowel and bladder had emptied hours ago, excremental bacteria colluding with tinkle, one neglected diaper wick white-lipped out to soak her sleepsuit and blanket her snuffled nose in deadly gas. Her limbs were listless. A long wrinkled thumb lay by one cheek, too far, too detached to move closer. Its nail bed and those of her curled fingers were tinged blue, as were her lips, sleep-sucking the sour nipple of a ghost breast, then quiescing, falling dormant, faint indraw and outflow of breath simply dropping off.

A cold gust of wind rattled the ground-floor window, but double-reinforced glass kept the Montreal winter out. A scatter of spicular snow swirled against it like tossed sand, then fell restless to the stone sill outside. Once more. And again.

Two minutes later, Jenny's daddy eased open her door and reared back at the rankness of the smell.

118

***

Travis eased open the door. The air in here was warm and close as always, but one good thing about that, Travis supposed, was that it concentrated the sweet baby smell of his daughter. He loved holding Jenny high on his chest so that he could caress her smooth pink cheeks with his nose. Now, as Laura followed him in and wrapped an arm about his waist, he contented himself with leaning over to watch his baby girl's tiny nostrils ride the pulse of life, the odor of crushed rose-petals sweetening the air about her.

"She's so beautiful," Laura said.

"Like her mother," said Travis, and Laura gave him a squeeze. Divorcing Carol, painful as the process had been for them both, and signing on as associate professor with McGill's Computer Science department, had been the wisest decisions he'd ever made. Never in the two decades since his first visit to Montreal had he felt so vividly alive. And now, with Laura so passionate and bright by his side and baby Jenny shining her marvelous light into his life, a sense of all-encompassing, all-infusing vitality filled him brimful with joy.

"Maybe I should give Marcie a call." Fret-voice.

"She'll be here," said Travis, glancing at his watch. "Seven-twenty. She's never late."

"I haven't seen her in three days. Have you?"

"No, but that's not—"

"What if something happened to her? She lives alone upstairs. Brings home those strange men since Pierre got booted out. Poor guy. I really thought he was the one."

"We're the one. You and I could make her very happy, and both of you know it."

"Shhh, you'll wake Jenny. You're such a tease. Come on, let's get our coats." Kissing a fingertip, Laura laid it lightly against the slumbering baby's cheek.

Travis closed the door softly after them. Laura gave him a hug and he brought her in for a deep slurpy kiss, an ever-renewed appreciation for her stifling smothering lips and tongue. Luscious lips, luscious labia to match, juicy as a warm ripe peach. He kissed her earlobe, swept inside her ear, made her moan. Tenderly, jokingly, he whispered, "Fucking you was the best thing I ever did."

"She's beautiful, isn't she?" Laura said, laughter in her voice. Travis was halfway to hard now and he knew his wife was dripping. "Maybe," she said, "we ought to try it again right now."

"Love to, but Marcie'll be here any moment and we'll be late for the swami." Carol had been an icicle. Laura was an oven, twenty-six and Canadian-hot, with the lovely sexual openness he'd known in Montreal from so many young women in the early seventies. He'd attended satsang then offered by Shyam and Satchitananda; she'd spent a month or two in Apadravya's makeshift ashram four years ago before the guru closed it down and returned to India. Computers and holy men had been the commonality that had brought him and Laura together into initial conversation. And now the swami, falsely rumored dead, had returned for one evening to begin an American tour, Laura's chance to renew an old tie and Travis's to experience the master in person.

Laura brought his hand up under her skirt, guided his thumb, coaxed it under the thigh-elastic of her panties so that, to the knuckle, it sank into the moist clench of her vulva and grew slick. "Fuck the swami, and fuck Marcie," she said, gyrating on his thumb.

"I'd take you up on half your proposition," he joked, but Laura had his belt undone and his zipper down and was tugging on his pants and briefs so that they fell to his knees and he sprang into the warm and eager caress of her hands.

Heaven's sakes! They must not have locked the front door nor heard Marcie's knock, for suddenly it flew open and there she stood, legs apart, in boots and bustier and crotchless panties, a riot of red hair bushed below and a double sweep above, crimson-tinted and silken-smooth and curled in twin licks about her upjutting nipples. "Well, well," she said, fists on hips, whip handle like a braided blacksnake erect in her right hand, "what yummies have we here?"

***

"She's beautiful, isn't she?" Laura said, laughter in her voice. She took his hand, about to say something else when they heard the stairs to the second-floor apartments creak and a clumsy someone stagger into the hallway.

"It's Marcie," he ventured.

"Doesn't sound like her." She broke away. "I'd know her footsteps anywhere. More like a slow-moving cripple, somebody with a bum leg, that sound."

Whoever it was stopped outside the door. There were fingernail scrapings swirling chest-high. Then the handle jump-rattled once-twice as if it were being sharply yanked upward, and when that stopped, muffled fists cottoned upon the door like distant booms of cannon fire.

"What the hell—?"

Laura laughed. "Remember Halloween a year ago? Her and Pierre coming down to get us for the costume party at Place des Arts?"

He relaxed. Flashed back upon him. "They pulled the same shit: lumbering and giggling, playing ghoul'n'zombie even after we opened the door, wrestling us to the rug."

"Precisely, though it's kinda morbid with Pierre gone and no giggling." Laura gave him a look. "Get the coats, honey. I'll let her in and give her some kind of hell for isolating herself three whole days."

Travis agreed. He was just at the hall closet, ready to tug it open and unhanger their long heavy fake-otterfur coats, when Laura said, "Okay, Marcie, you sick puppy of a neighbor," and pulled open the door.

The sight struck him and then the smell, a subliminal skirl of stench curled around the doorframe moments before and now fully bloomed into a gut-wrenching skunk-and-offal stew. It was Marcie, and yet it couldn't be: Her yellow terrycloth robe hung loose and open like old drapes yanked back from a window onto hell. Above the bloat and sewage of her flesh, the eyes in her creamed face were dead egg-yolk eyes, and yet they moved, swimming sentient yolks in colloidal pus. Her

121

hair hugged like wet parentheses about her head, and her hands lifted (they *lifted*, unspeakable act) seemingly to wrench at the draped strands. One found its foul bell-pull, but the other shot out and grabbed at Laura, gripping its puffy fingers at her nape and pulling her off-balance toward a gaping maw.

"No!" he said, no air behind it. He was as paralyzed as Laura had been, half hero, half coward, and completely a shock in the shape of a man. By the time he made up his mind to move, the bloated Marcie's teeth had scraped deep gouges in Laura's face, nose and mouth crammed inside the creature's jaws, her hands pushing without effect against dead breasts, her eyes a horse's eyes in terror all teary and looking back at him. Her muffled screams grew louder and clearer as Marcie's jaws closed and pulled and yanked away her skull-cover, front teeth crunching and crumbling into the moist chew. As Travis came on, the blood-soaked thing worked bits of his wife's face into its cheeks, let cheek-flesh hang loose from its mouth like pizza toppings, but (surprising strength) grabbed the hand he raised to it and stuffed it gullet-deep, coming down, breaking skin and bone, turning spattered egg-yolk eyes on him as, no longer heroic, he tried to free his flesh from the mangling vise and yelled louder and more ineffectual than he'd ever done in any nightmare.

Through his pain, he saw Madame Robichaux, groceries in hand and oblivious to what was going on, fumble her key into the inner door by the mailboxes.

"Must be Marcie," ventured Travis.

"Not her usual spry step," his wife observed.

"Losing a lover takes a lot out of anyone," he said, and, as if in affirmation, Marcie's familiar rap sounded, but slower and less sprightly than usual. "I'll get it," he said. "Bring the coats, okay?"

He turned the deadbolt and opened the door. Marcie stood there, one arm behind her back. Striking redhead, her love-scent clinging to his mustache from their lunch hour together, Marcie gliding the rubber Metro back here from the symphony office, flumpfing down naked, raw, and ready on her bed, crying for Pierre as Travis roused her, but he didn't mind, not with the vulnerable taste of her sex filling his mouth and the way her coming brought his name to her lips as Marcie sheathed him, stabbing at his eyes with that voracious hunger of hers.

"Hi, Marcie." How obscenely normal he sounded, how hollow. Past the mailboxes, Madame Robichaux was coming through the vestibule door, juggling bulgy grocery bags.

"Have you told her yet?" High-strung, a taut steel wire toe-gripped, every muscle working against tilt.

"Marcie, why don't you—?"

"Told me what?" Laura had the coats folded over her arms like wheat sheaves. He barely glanced at her, but it was enough to see recognition glimmer and flit, denial her first impulse. Again to Marcie. Love was so complicated. He wanted both these amazing ladies, but if he were forced to choose, he preferred, truth to tell, Marcie's passion, her quirky big-boned ways, the refreshing raft of musical friends she brought with her, a far cry from Laura's Bell Canada dullards. But there was the baby to consider; not his idea, true, but a daughter was a daughter, no matter how you sliced it, and he—

Marcie shot daggers at him, then turned to Laura, and he saw Madame Robichaux's eyes widen at what Marcie's hand gripped behind her back, even as it was coming around, the movie glint surely imagined, but it flashed by so fast and sank into Laura's chest, right above her armload of coats, faltering blood-parabola darkening the fur as she fell and Marcie shouting, "He's mine!", turning then to chase down a hapless neighbor frozen in place but then bolting, her two bags of food absurdly clutched to her and slowing her down so that the knife hilting into her back sprang her arms up and open and celery stalks and egg cartons flew like birds alarmed out of the bag-rustle of her flushed life.

In her apartment on Rue Peel, between l'Avenue des Pins and Docteur-Penfield, Aysha sat grieving by her dead son Vish. Three years old, looking hurt and bewildered in his high delirium, Vish had had his father's dark eyes, if none of his realized serenity. Her fault, that. Her year in the ashram, becoming Rajib's preferred wife in his last months here, had done nothing to conquer the unquenchable ego-longings in her. They still plagued her, despite her ongoing efforts to purify herself, and they'd given Vish, who deserved better coming from such seed, not the quiet mirror that suited him, but a restless, breeze-perturbed, disease-inducing, Western jitteriness. High fever, food and drink refused, all her natural remedies for naught— and all she could do was watch Vish dwindle and die, her tears for him a weakness she despised, even as she cried them.

The shutters accordioned over his window rattled as a gust of wind shook the glass. The oil lamp's flame danced in its glass chimney, then settled. It reassured her, as it always did when she meditated on it—not the pasteboard reassurance of the material world, but a true soothe from her inner depths. Surely, it said, Vish's dying, arriving as it did on the day of Rajib's return, was an irrefutable unmistakable sign. And that was particularly so given the report, six months past, of his death and burial in India, and now the rumors that he had returned, like Christ long ago, from the grave. If that were true, these rumors of resurrection, it might well be that Rajib would pass his hand over the boy, his unknown son, and flood the breath back into his airless lungs. It might well be that Vish would once again unlid his eyes and, in the calm depth of his father's love, find his way swiftly to nirvana.

Aysha raised the old watch she'd put away years ago, held it close to the light, saw that soon they would need to be on their way.

He turned the deadbolt and opened the door. Marcie stood there, one arm behind her back.

"Well, look who's here," he said.

"Hello, you two," she said, bouncing in behind a huge grin and whipping out a wrapped gift. "A little something for my two favorite people in the world." Juggling a pair of grocery bags, Madame Robichaux finagled her way through the vestibule door.

Laura came up with the coats. "Jeez, you didn't have to do that." Her eyes bubbled and brimmed. Lovely Laura, the Canada Dry of his life. "Open it, Travis," she said. "Okay, okay. Hardly guess what it is." Marcie gave his shoulder a playful punch as he unribboned the telltale rectangular shape and husked the wrapping paper off. "My boss's latest." Maestro Dutoit's face, a skilled musician and an engaging personality from the brief hello they'd shared with him at the opening night reception that fall. "Tchaikovsky's Sixth," Laura read aloud. Marcie nodded. "Good crying music," she said. A raw twist to her tossed-off words gave his heart a twinge. "Come here, Marcie love," he said, gathering his upstairs neighbor's big-boned body to him. Laura let fall the coats in a floomph to the floor and joined in a three-way hug. "You're so sweet and good and giving, the world owes you a good long cry-free zone, and if you can't find that upstairs, you just come down here any time. It'll be waiting right here." Marcie's eyes were moist. "I love you both so much," she said, planting a huge soft kiss on his cheek and then dipping down to cover half of Laura's petite face with her lips. What a turn-on these two women were. If he weren't blessed with dear Laura, he would surely, he thought, make a play for Marcie. Passionate thing. He fancied she'd be the sort to take the initiative more frequently than Laura did, surprising him with silky nothings, stripping for his delectation to sultry music, cherrying those luscious lips about his arousal and deepening downward.

Laura broke the embrace first, a fluster in her ways. Madame Robichaux went past on the way to her apartment, an odd look on her rubbery face. "Bonjour, Henriette," Laura sang out and after a pause, the woman's answering "'jour," clipped and suspicious, came floating back.

Travis placed the jewelbox on a small drop-down table near the door and rustled up the coats from the floor. He held Laura's for her, then shouldered his own on, as Laura jabbered inanely about where things were, how often Marcie was to look in on Jenny, how late they thought they'd be, where (for God's sakes

125

yet again) the diapers and the pins and the formula and the bottles were. For some reason, he could not catch her eyes as she gabbled. Overprotective, hyper, even paranoid—that's the way Laura had been about Jenny from the first, dressing her too warmly, leaving the thermostat on way too high, fussing interminably over her face and clothes when she held her. But something beyond nervousness was working at Laura now. And when he tested his puzzlement on Marcie, the flat plane of her gaze told him she knew what it was, that they were *both* holding back from him, and that Laura was ready to spill something that made Marcie at least mildly uncomfortable.

". . . oh, and in case of emergency, I've put a signed medical form on the kitchen table. You know where to find us, and . . . oh shit, Marcie, I know it's not a good time but it never seems to be a good time, please can't we tell him now, it's—"

"Tomorrow. Now you two go and have a good time—"

"Tell me what?" The air felt odd. Were they hiding a great gift, a bludgeon, what?

"Take a hike, ya lousy swami-lovers," said Marcie in her best tough-guy voice, hustling them toward the door, "or the baby buys it." God she smelled great, her sweet strong face set off by her chop-cut red hair, new kind of tai-kwon-do affectation, but it looked great on her. And he loved being strong-armed by her; what a wrestler she'd be bare-naked, the full spread of her huge firm breasts a treat in teased evasion, her flexed oiled thighs coming up and about to encuntify his mouth, to force him to feast as she devoured him below, parting her labia nose-deep around his nasal wedge and—

"Marcie and I are lovers."

With barely a hitch, Marcie freed him, veering Laura off to the right. "Now you've done it," she said.

His mind went umpteen ways, putting together dropped hints, unanswered phones, misinterpreted looks. Confusion passed. Elation lit and flared. "Oh, but that's—!"

"No!" Laura's voice exploded through her sobs. "You don't . . . he doesn't . . . ." She grabbed breath, riding its blast. "You're out of it . . . it's just Marcie and me . . . and the baby, I'm taking her with me."

Marcie seemed put off by Laura's display, even as she put a protective, supportive arm about her. In the baby's room, Jenny cried sharply as if a safety pin had opened to stab her out of sleep.

"Take a hike, ya lousy swami-lovers," said Marcie in her best George Raft, "or the baby buys it."

Laura blurted out, "Marcie's pregnant."

Marcie veered Laura off, then with overblown disgust and genuine dismay: "Jeez, you had to tell him."

"Well I think it's great," his wife protested, "and I'm sorry—I won't tell anyone else!—but I just couldn't keep it from Travis one second longer."

"Marcie, that's incredible," he said, going after her to catch her in a hug. He was amazed at his thoughts. He wished the child were his, though his lovely neighbor had, God damn her eyes, rebuffed his one early advance and had never invited a return attempt; he wondered which ungodly creep it was, or whether—and he imagined that this would be worse for her— it had been Pierre, in one of his final dribble-shots into her; he saw instantly their households fusing, him as her Lamaze coach, loving her child, as she and Laura did likewise, and welcoming her inevitably into their marriage bed.

Then, two feet shy of an embrace, the baby screamed. It was not a troubled whine ready to lapse as soon as it began, nor was it even a wide-awake startle and wail that required backpats and pacings-about and soothings before she could be replaced in her bassinet. No, these sounds meant sudden pain or upset, a slipped pin rolled over on, or something worse.

Laura reached the door first but he was close behind and felt the blast of frigid air over the incessant whine of the space heater. He saw the window thrown wide and a lingering glove gripping the casing and then gone, flings of slush still flying through the air from a disappearing boot. Race to the sill, past the empty bassinet, Laura's misgivings about a first-floor apartment replaying in his head, and there, through the diminishing squit-squit-squit of boots on snow and the wrenching wails of his child, he saw her kidnapper,

127

her white-slaver, dwindling swiftly in the ill-lit alley, pools of light by backdoors, dumpsters lined along brick walls. "Catch him, catch him!" Laura's hands were shoving him over the sill, almost throwing him off balance, but he kept his eye on the nightmare, so that just as he found his feet and felt the cold seep up inside his pantleg and was poised to run, he saw their ski-masked nemesis look back even as two shadows emerged from the dun of a dumpster and shudder-halted him so jarringly that his boots went awry and his bundle of baby flew into the hands of a slighter third figure. Saved, thought Travis, elated as Laura and Marcie joined him out the window. But then, instead of beating the man into submission, they appeared in the dim light to be pushing their heads against him so that he jittered and screamed as though electrified. And the third carried Jenny into the light, and he saw a meat-slung jawbone and a wandering eye and his daughter brought like some corncob to that mouth; and her sleepsuit bunched and reddened, her cries punched quiet from her, as, behind them, packed snow squeaked and Travis turned too late.

Laura reached the door first but he was close behind and took in the overheated room, the space heater humming at full capacity as Laura lifted Jenny into her arms.

"She okay?" Marcie asked.

Laura nodded, arching her back and soothing the tiny face open wide in terror at her shoulder, features almost lost in the laced, peaked, buttoned sleepsuit-head.

"Must've been gas pains," he said.

Laura replaced the baby in her bassinet, zip-slashing the zipper, reaching in to feel diaper, rezipping, kissing one mittened hand. Travis was starting to sweat, the room was so hot and his heavy coat was meant for fierce cold.

"Diaper's a smidge damp, but she'll be fine."

The baby sneezed but her lid-heavy eyes did not open. Her lips parted for air, a soft pooch of pink budding. No more than two dark dots, her nostrils.

"Poor baby has the sniffles," Laura said and pointed them toward the door. The instant it closed behind them, Jenny's face winced as if to scream again, but her bowels and bladder gave way then, emptying, and her face relaxed into sleep. Where Laura had felt for sop, a lip of cotton bridged between the freshly soaked diaper beneath plastic pants and the layers of cloth working outward to the soon-to-be-ammoniated sleepsuit.

"Say," said Marcie, "hadn't you two better be on your way?"

Travis checked his wrist. Quarter to eight. "We're a brisk ten-minute walk away, so we're cutting it close, I guess. One last hug, Marcie dear. Mmmmwah! What a woman you are." Her kiss lingered like a warm slap on his lips.

Laura began: "Now don't forget to—"

Marcie swept his compact woman up in a tremendous hug and stopped her frettings with a kiss, short, startling to them both, not wet. "Hmm," she said, "what an interesting impulse."

"Hold that thought," Travis said. "If Apadravya can no longer strut his stuff, we may be back quicker than we expect, ready to explore other paths to salvation."

Laura's eyes still held shock. "Help yourself to the fridge. Nothing's off-limits." She brightened, kept back from saying something, then tugged him out the door. Try as he might, Travis couldn't shake two contrary feelings: that something very wonderful awaited them at the end of a very wonderful evening; and that venturing out tonight was a terrible mistake, one they might not live long enough to regret.

As she dressed her dead son, Aysha only kept herself from coming apart by holding Rajib's eyes centrally before her. She had had to call him Swami Apadravya when others were about; but alone in the quiet calm of his room, dark hands sculpting her white flesh, he was her Rajib, loving her so totally it hurt. And when he entered her, his eyes a searing mirror of bliss, the world split open anew until she thinned and thickened into slow explosion.

Vish lay cold under her fingers. As she joggled his body, she expected any moment he'd inhale suddenly out of sleep, find his thumb, offer a long protesting groan, and eye her archly. But the chill of his skin and its pallor, like an all-over faint, kept his death at her fingertips. Underwear, undershirt, tight white socks, futile nonsense, must be insane, long corduroy pants, a pullover shirt with dead arms atangle around a halfwit's lolled head that made her break down weeping—until Rajib's eyes, cased in quiet brown wrinkles and containing the wisdom and compassion of all the world, brought her out of it. Sweater played his arms the same way, but by the time she rocked his coat on, it was like dressing a weighty ragdoll, both her and Vish more insulated from his death. But no. Had to experience it, had to keep it before her like a candleflame. Visions required faith, and faith could only function in the harsh light of the truth. She would carry her boy to his father and he would interrupt satsang—or rather, he would surely incorporate her arrival into what he was saying (no agenda that excluded the world's surprises) and then Rajib would touch his son, re-blood his cream-tan skin, re-bellow his lungs, infuse through the eyes his resurrected boy. But no. She couldn't count on that. "Make no appointments," he had said, "receive no disappointments." Why was that such hard advice to follow?

Aysha zipped up her boots, then muffled her neck and double-buttoned her night-blue coat. She jammed the knit cap down on her flattened blond curls and, Vish's pillow cold against her knuckles, worked his cap over his scalp and down around the tops of his ears. She blew out the oil-lamp and stagger-lifted her son until he was snugged on her left arm and his head rested against her shoulder. Would be a test of her will, this walk: five blocks west and nearly as distant south; no new snow for two days but brisk winds, and there'd be snowbanks and patches of snow between scraped sidewalks. She prayed she'd meet no one on the way out of her apartment building, and that proved true. A blast of air, caution on the icy concrete of her front steps, and she was on her way.

The moment they cornered off Drummond and headed west on Maisonneuve, Travis sensed something wrong. They were still three blocks from Sir George Williams University, a mostly evening school in one several-story building where the talk was to be held. Couldn't guess what it was as he and Laura crunched along, her enthusing about their baby's precocity as he tuned her out—but it increasingly nagged at him and then turned to disappointment. Volumetrically speaking, pedestrian traffic was too light: a first sign. And when they crossed Crescent and had a clear view of the corner of Bishop and Maisonneuve ahead, Laura interrupted her parental ravings with an "Oh shoot!"

Save for security lights on the central stairs and on the walkways left and right around them to the auditorium, the building was dark. "Look at this!" Laura said, and he joined her at the glass doors. Her hands were thrust into her coat pockets; she jiggled from the cold and her breath was dragon steam, comical from her Cupid's-bow lips. Upon the door, taped askew on the inside, was a pasteboard sign in bold black: SATSANG POSTPONED UNTIL NEXT WEEKEND. SRI APADRAVYA IS THE LIGHT OF THE WORLD. NAMASTE.

"Didn't you check the paper?" she asked, accusing.

"Yesterday's." He caressed the back of her coat with his thick gloved fingers. "Hey, no big deal. We'll go to the Cafe Au Lait, have some steamy roasted coffee and that honey-drenched dessert you like."

"Baklava."

"Right."

"I had my heart set on a little spiritual well-being tonight, not to mention seeing old friends from the ashram and Apadravya himself." Laura leaned her forehead against his shoulder-fur in mock sorrow.

"Make no appointments—"

"I know, you doofus, I know."

And that's when, with a shadowed crowd of pedestrians penguining oddly toward them south on Bishop, twin snicks of metal sounded behind them and two burly men yanked them apart and brought sharp blades and faces impossibly close. "Your wallet in two seconds, sucker, or you're dead," and as much as Travis wanted to look after Laura and the other mugger, the hopped-up urgency in the man's eyes went right to Travis's nervous system, the arm, the hand, tearing off a glove to reach between the lower buttons of his coat, to lip the heavy fabric back, an inconsequential drag on his wrist as he gripped and drew out his black eelskin wallet, no shake in his hand, no time for fear, too much a luxury when faced with that much need.

And then the smell of death stung him. His own? Had he been slashed? But his assailant's eyes bulged as Laura screamed, and still he lived. His wallet fell. A purpled foot toed forward and Travis saw a matching hand jam down, like a receipt on a spindle, upon the switchblade, fingers closing on the mugger's glove, a sharp snap of bone. Time enough to feel blooms of gratitude mixed with astonishment before the rescuer dropped his head upon Travis's shoulder and bit, as easy as baklava, through the thick fur, thick leather, the multi-layered cloth beneath, into muscle and bone, a sudden frenzied cramp of pain there.

The moment they cornered off Drummond and headed west on Maisonneuve, anticipation lit his soul. They quickened their pace, he and Laura, grinning like idiots. "Namaste, dollface," he said, side-hugging her as they walked.

Laura, laughing, scolded: "That's not nice, making fun of spirituality."

"Get me started on Jesus sometime."

"I know, I know. My favorite blasphemer."

Inside, the crowd was lumbering along the guideropes, halfway vestibuled, halfway inside the auditorium: an odd mingle of young and old, his generation touching once more a thread which guided them to the gold of an earlier time, Laura's coevals refreshingly glint-eyed in their twentyish claim upon the world's possibilities. On their way to the line's end, Laura exchanged joyous if hushed hellos with a number of young men and women he'd never met, scrubbed and more naive-looking than his wife, wearing yoga-whites some of them and holding coats, although, inching past the side door they'd come in, blasts of winter assaulted them every time anyone entered the building.

At last the double doors. Travis let Laura unpurse a five-dollar bill for them and place it on a small mound of money in a box labeled DONATIONS. He took a flyer about a potluck, avoiding the fervid eyes of the redeemed druggie, or so he appeared, sitting, one knee pistoning, behind the table.

"Let's try close," Laura said, ever one for ring-side seats at plays and concerts.

"Right," he said, but she was already on the way down the carpeted slope of the aisle. She tapped the sweatered arm of a petite Oriental woman, blowing a kiss to her wave and signaling *later* as she backwarded and then rightwarded herself toward the sparsely populated—because spiritually too presumptuous?—front rows.

The air was redolent with incense, sandalwood mingled with a fruity vanilla scent. The stage, as he approached it, brought him back twenty years, the oriental rug at its lip, fringe hanging over, the cushions, the flowers, puffs of incense rising nearly straight up like Lionel trains in mid-chug from an ornately carved table—and out of context yet never somehow out of place, the angled mike on a squat stand so that the reputedly soft-spoken Apadravya could be heard throughout the auditorium and so that his talk could be preserved for those unlucky enough to be elsewhere.

Laura draped her coat over her seatback in row two, a clack as a button brushed metal. He did the same, gazing back at the rising sweep of attendees, noting how animated their faces were, yet how subdued their chatter. This, he thought, was how church ought to be but never was.

"You're really going to like him, Travis."

Sweet woman, her face so vibrant and alive. "I like him already," he said, and gave Laura a squeeze.

Marcie hummed as she bumsteaded her sandwich, habits both she'd picked up from her father, a man chubby-not-fat who favored a puttering hum over silence in the car. Hand on meat drawer, drew it open, packaged sliced turkey ready for unsealing; salami, the same; tuppered ham on one shelf still looking worthy; lettuce head with a few hacks out of it, snatched

133

up; jars of mayo and dill spears precariously balanced at her breasts. She brought her armful of prizes to the table, arrayed them, and dove in, rye slices peeled open waiting on the plate.

As her hands worked, she wondered if she should check on baby Jenny. Time enough for that later. Laura, lovely pert-nosed Laura, was such a hoverer, it would probably do the kid good to suffer a little neglect. She and Travis'd moved in, going on two years now, and it had been a relief and a blessing after the beer-guzzling, once-overing, trio of scum-buddies who'd lived here before. They'd been away at a hockey game in Toronto the weekend Pierre brought her here and had committed them to a lease.

Pierre again. Bring him up, even fleetingly, and his residue lingered and spread, reviving the sweet and bitter ache of times buried and buried and buried again. Stopped over the table, knife in hand, kitchen clock relentless in its forward hurtle. Brought up Freya Cole, leggy sad-eyed sandy-haired first-chair violist she had found solace with for a while: a quiet, caressive time, very few words, two lives lived, one here in seeming isolation, one there idle and indolent on Freya's bed, her Scandinavian fingers sure and angular and rich drawing tone from her viola, then dry and light and loving on Marcie's freshly inflicted wounds. It died away. Trombonist dork Kyle Kinney pursued his pet violist with bizarre gifts, won her, took them both off to Chicago under Maestro Solti's baton.

Hey, what could you do? Heartache sucked, and there were plenty of people out there willing to leech off your grief. Go on, sniff the air, keep your bullshit detector in fresh batteries: That was the way to get by.

Stupid lump stood in her throat. Wasn't fair. If she were a drinking woman, she'd be drunk. Instead, she lifted the triple-decker to her lips, opened her mouth as wide as it would go, and chomped the biggest bite of meat and bread and bitter sorrow she could manage.

He left-armed Laura's coat-bulged seatback and craned about to scan the crowd. Odd how gatherings culled from a city this size a mini-population of like-minded souls. He felt (grand illusion, that) immediate kinship here; rebuke followed instantly, no call for cynicism, there *could* be a grand gathering of these same people, one massive handfast to bind them all, spark to spark—enduring fascination and interest here, if they wanted it enough. These people, he fancied, lived, like him at his best, aside and apart from the weary fray of illusion, not tangled up in the snags of samsara, or not often, or with sufficient awareness to put a spin of redemptive humor on the human predicament.

"Elephant-shitting again?" Laura asked, knuckling his left temple playfully.

Fritz Perls' term. "Yep."

"Know you pretty well, don't I?"

"What can I say?" Travis returned her smile. "I'm an outie, you're an innie."

It was enough. Laura tucked her cross-legged ankles tighter under her buttsplit, rocking to rectify them, and rested her hands, palm up and thumb-to-index-finger, upon her knees. Seemed affected to him, but what the hell, if it got her through the night, it was good.

He observed the trickle of aisle activity, new folks scanning or pointing or scarf-sweeping their hunched-over, side-swaggling, pardon-my-heels-on-your-toes way toward a brass-ring grab at enlightenment. Man four rows back was scratching his face, listening to a companion. A cluster of incandescent young women, mid-auditorium, set his mind-cock afrisking for an instant, then he veered off them in deference to their privacy and on to a couple of executive types, glint-eyed from the backglow of money in their day-to-day lives, he thought, Jacob Needleman readers who were easy straddling both worlds.

A quick movement, or jarring. The man scratching his face looked sallow, no great complexion to begin with, but his scratching wasn't helping any. His fingernails seemed to be tracing welts from cheek to jaw, but then Travis saw runnels of blood down to the first knuckle and realized he wasn't seeing welts but gouges and that they weren't being traced but opened. When the man's glance started to shift forward,

Travis took quick refuge in the cluster of cuties further back. But now their skin too, which had blushed a lively vivacity like reddish glows on golden apples, slung wan and dead from fish-glimmered eyes. Feeling the spread come down like a wave of sun over a windy field, he turned to shield himself and his woman from the impact; but Laura whiffed into his nostrils, and Laura clutched his arm, and Laura quick-leaned her puffed purple face, its reeky mouth glistening open, in toward his neck.

Moving from the wise old executives to the scratcher, he wondered if the fellow had a thing about his face. Did he unwax his earholes with an idle pinkie? Did he pry out boogers when no one was about, or chisel up layers of dead skin beneath his hair, opening and tormenting scalp wounds as his body mounted a slow steady assault upon itself?

Laura nudged him. He looked her way and she eyed him toward the stage. There was a stirring at the curtain off stage right. Then a tall blond-bearded man in Deva pants, whom Travis had seen somewhere before, came out far enough to step backward into the heavy red billow of the curtain, making way for the short Indian man who ambled out, hands cupped prayerfully before him as he walked. The tall man seemed stricken, though Travis couldn't tell if his state reflected agony or ecstasy.

Seats flipped up behind them in the auditorium. His wife dug into her coat pocket and brought forth the baggie of rose petals she'd plucked from a bought bouquet an hour before. They went out her side, him feeling a little like a fool following her. Someone from McGill saw him, they'd hound him forever. Well, fuck 'em. Anybody in a position to see him was as blackmailable as he was. Laura put some petals in his palm and for the next many seconds, the tall air was filled with silent tiddlywink flurries of pink and white and red petals, flinging up and drifting down around the holy man's upstretched arms and face. When the gentle rain was done, he lowered them and Travis had a first good glimpse of his eyes. No one there, everyone there, a guru trick he'd seen before but never like this: the dark dead glint hinted of tarnished brass, and behind it lay at once the calm of total resignation and assent and the agitation of a star about to go nova. But he couldn't be certain of that—it was one of the things he liked about Indian fakir types—and the man's gaze had made its profound impression on him and moved on.

Hands thrust past Travis's either shoulder stretched out to touch the swami. Devotees lightly laughed as they leaned by him to touch the moving hand. A few arms pulled away, a few laughs died on the vine, but mostly it was an ineffable grasp at joy. Travis figured what the hell, who was he to hold back. He leaned out, Laura's patient white palm next to his, and two dark hands gripped them and held for an instant. Travis focused on the hands, riveting his attention there: not the dry healthy brown he'd expected, but a slick grayish-khaki like ground round just beginning to move off raw-red on a grill; translucent amber droplets oozed from back-hand pores, tree sap on bark, and the oily heat around his gripped hand suggested the holy man exuded from his palms as well. Travis looked faceward. Towelled off, perhaps, before he hit the stage, the brow and cheeks now, like saturated sponges, obtruded pinpricks of oil, as numerous as beads of flopsweat. The eyes, though: Behind them lay that same cosmic struggle, but just as the guru's firm grip passed over into discomfort and the static greet of contact turned to tug, Travis realized that composure's hold was crumbling in those eyes.

But by then it was too late. Whether it was some odd attraction about the two of them that set him off, or just the luck of the draw, the wiry lightweight deadweight holy man pulled them, kneecaps slammed hard on stage-edge, over the upflipped rug and inexorably toward his hungry gape of a mouth.

His hands left theirs. Travis's palm tingled. As he withdrew it, he pooled his ring finger into the exudate at his lifeline, a substance as thick as honey but not sticky or unpleasant in any way. Returning to his seat, Laura at his side, he sniffed his finger and thought of coconut oil slicked on moist pussy.

137

Laura took his other hand beneath the end of the seat-arm that separated them, giving him an odd look; her fingers slid lubriciously where they grasped him, assuring him and being assured.

Onstage, Apadravya was nodding and smiling, getting a sense of the room, taking its measure.

Laura tugged his arm. "He's not breathing," came her taut whisper as he lowered his ear to her.

He eyebrowed her, turning his attention back to stage center. Nonsense. The man was breathing. Had to be. He knew Laura was dead right, knew it like the flare of truth in a night of lies. Beneath the unsettled counterpoise of peace and Armageddon in his eyes had been this unsettling, unobserved other phenomenon: no breath, no om, no shanti. Days gone by, Shyam or Satchitananda would bring the crowd together with shared chants, shared breathing. That would have begun by now, if it was going to happen at all.

Ripples of laughter took the hall. Not nervous, just the delight of those deep and innocent souls who know that the guru turns time into timelessness, teaching impatience to cease, wordlessly wise before satsang begins.

The blond-bearded yoga teacher set a filled glass and a pitcher of water on a tray near Apadravya. A dismissive glance gave it and him invisibility. On the periphery, he slunk away. The pitcher, the glass, remained untouched as long as Travis and Laura remained in the auditorium.

Apadravya's eyes scanned the hall.

Any moment now he would speak.

Any moment now.

Marcie wolfed into her sandwich. Couldn't taste the fucker worth shit. *Chew your food*, mama voice gentle from Winnipeg, fancied recollections of warm tit in her mouth, an overwhelming plane of flesh, Pierre's penis swallowed past the gag reflex, dim ringlets of private hair like a sneeze tickling her nose. The back of her throat took a wrong turn in mid-swallow, and suddenly there was no air.

She dropped the sandwich, top lettuced slice falling

off and bouncing like a mattress hurtling out a window to concrete below. Her chair scraped. Her hands flew to her neck, overlapping V's like mercy-me, and she staggered to the sink. Disposal side, already picturing the vomit but better here than on their floor; a cereal bowl, its spoon in water, unclog the windpipe, get air in, wash the sucker off after. But leaning over, willing expulsion, thrusting her fingers deep inside her mouth as blood oceaned in her head, had no effect. No time for cops, even if she could communicate with them. She jammed her abdomen against the sink edge, absurdly worrying about the baby growing there. Again and again, punish the body, wake it up, get it to do the right thing, oh yeah, windpipe blocked, jig this n jog that n she'll be good as new, sorry for any trouble ma'am. But the outrage persisted and the saliva dribbled from her lips to the sink below, and the air was not there, and not there, and *not there*. Flat patches of black cloth dimpled on the periphery of her vision, then the sink edge slipped upward, eluding her fingers, and the flat hard palm of the floor, dull wool, coldly smacked her.

"In Muslim tradition," his quiet voice rode unneeded intakes and outflows of air, disturbing at first to Travis but then quickly mesmerizing, "King Solomon died in this fashion: By means of a magic ring, he enslaved the djinn, the demons, and made them build his temple. Leaning upon a long staff, he stood there as they worked, his wise gray head bowed in meditation, for days at a time. Still they toiled, the gleam of Solomon's ring calling to mind their enslavement."

Laura squeezed his hand. He could feel her disquiet, her thrill, without looking at her. He felt it too. This man, sitting not ten feet from them, showing every sign of sentience and launching satsang with some sort of parable, was not quite alive. Travis could almost see the suck of gravedirt on him, his body emerged from earthgrip just far enough to hide its hold on him. He embrowned the flowers around him, the pillows, the patterned rug. The movement of his facial muscles was minimal, sufficient to bear his message but no more—and this was not the just-enough of a living holy man, though closely akin, but the articulated willed urge of once-living flesh to reclaim its place and find in reassembly its fix on vitality.

"One day, Solomon came out and stood where he always stood, propped up by his staff, head lowered for nearly a year, unmoved. And in the same year, a white worm gnawed its way up inside the staff, eating, eating, hollowing it out until it was a shell. The djinn worked, not daring to interrupt Solomon in his involutions, and the temple was finished. At the moment the final brick was mortared and the work done, the staff could no longer bear the king's weight. And so he fell. And the djinn discovered that he had been dead for an entire year, though his body had not, in all that time, corrupted in any way, so right and good and blessed a person this good King Solomon had been."

Marcie started. Disorientation, like a hot nap ended on a bad note. And a great gape of need. Tangle of limbs moving, cabinetry blurring by, a fleeting realization that she was rising, but no memory stuck and there was movement only. Toward the satisfaction of her need. Fixtures went by, hanging beaters and spatulas, door frame, wall photos, light switch. Caught on a couch end, room sweeping like a fan, then a righting, and onward again.

Veer left, dark here but no matter. Buffered against flat cool something, a barrier. Dim wispings of some easy way past it, but it was flimsy stuff, a loud cottony noise as it splintered inward and gave and duddered aside. Odor of need, food call in the hot dark place—dancing mushroom spun by, foreskin, gone. Threaded the sound. Groped down to find it, found it, lifted it, twisted the right side to tear some off, sharp crack and sharp increase in the sound of its need to be taken in. Lolling leftward, the exposed part, pure scent of noise and the stuff she craved. Shuck of her jaws opening, tight skin dry and protesting. Noise lowered like a dream, yes, yes, jaws closing, toothscrape, the hot fluids freshening the dryness in her mouth, a wash over face, the noise still pulsing but abruptly out as she munched past the bony part and tore the yellow batting off to go further.

***

The holy man paused. And Travis swore that what sat on the stage was little more than a corpse. But then the head moved and the hands clasped one another on his robed lap and Travis heard the unneeded (but for speech) insuck of breath.

"Certain holy saints, it is thoroughly documented in Roman Catholic records," his head nodded as he spoke, and his grave eyes twinkled like mica, "lived such pure lives that even in death they did not bloat or decay, preserved in some cases for centuries. Saint Angela Merici died in the year 1540. In 1672, her body was found to be intact, incorrupt, sweet smelling. And again in 1867, they found the same incorruption."

Inside, Travis felt disoriented yet not disturbed, a quiet rush that satsang always brought but weirdly warped, and yet nothing less than fascinating. He felt as if he ought to want to bolt, yet he felt perfectly safe and, in an odd way, holy, to be sitting near this whatever-he-was balanced on a crest of oblivion, conveying its message.

"Eleven years following the death of Saint Camillus de Lellis, at his official recognition for sainthood, his exhumed body was as fresh and supple as in life; fragrant liquids exuding from him were referred to as copious. So too with Saint John of the Cross, whose flesh was found to be incorrupt for more than two and a half centuries." The holy man let it sink in. His eyes scanned the crowd, then fixed for a soul-searing moment on Travis, before lifting lightly away like a mosquito refraining from puncture and suck.

On the north slope of Mount Royal, in La Cimetière de Notre-Dame-des-Neiges, Huguette thrust gloveless hands into her fleecy coat pockets and shifted uncomfortably from one boot to the other, waiting for her idiot boyfriend. Chill air was seeping its way under her coat, spiraling up where clothing ought to be protecting her, but where instead, at Louis-Phillipe's insistence, she wore nothing at all. The English spoke of freezing your ass off; now she knew first hand—and wished she didn't—what that phrase meant.

141

This was stupid. Black Angel with her head bowed and her hands angled open at her sides, thumb-tops dusted with snow: he had said it was good luck to make love under her gaze, but Huguette suspected it was just one more excuse to have sex in an odd locale. Why not? She was finally free of her parents. They were crazy in love. And she had to admit, for all her discomfort and in spite of the shocking overtones of making love in this place—her *grandmère*, she had to keep reminding herself, was buried not two hundred yards away—she was turned on at the thought of his impish grin backlit, over the blanket she'd brought, by the black sculpted frown of the Angel. Looked awfully thin, spread out on the ground, that blanket.

Then she saw Louis-Phillipe coming from the direction of l'Université de Montreal below, sleeping bag rolled up under one arm. He lurched among tombstones and she hugged herself and jiggled, shouting for him to hurry. Crunching to her, he gave her a huge warm kiss, then untied the bag and unzipped it open atop the blanket. While he was busy, she bit the bullet, unbuttoning her coat and flinging past him onto her back, coat a third layer but bare naked above except for her arms. These she lifted. *"Vite, vite,"* she said. "Cover me, I'm freezing." Her nips were tight with cold and her slick *chatte* tingled with winter wet.

He jittered his fingers down his coat, unbuttoning to expose himself, raw red funny-finger upjutting, then flew down upon her in a rush of cold. Squirming on her: "Take that side, I'll do this." He fumbled his buttons into her holes by her left thigh, while she struggled with the ones on the right, laughing with him as, farther up, it became impossible, arms atangle; but with all the squirming, he'd slipped the yummy tip of his thickness inside her, and the body heat was intense enough that she coaxed his lips down to hers and slow-groined more of his love inside her.

Startled upward. Broke the kiss: "It looks like the Angel is about to fall on us," she said.

Louis-Phillipe laughed. And then they heard shuffled boots from behind the Black Angel. His head craned up as hard white faces under knit caps bobbled through the black night. Hands wrenched him off her, his penis slipping out and exposing her. She tried to cover up, but boots jammed down on her shoulders. "Hey, guys, lookie here. Anybody wanna fuck a frog? Nice froggie, ribbit, ribbit, ribbit." Mittened fingers tweaked her right nipple and she smacked them away, but they jammed between her thighs and roughly thrust inside. "Placeholder, assholes. First pecker out gets to go first."

"Get away from me!" she screamed, as Louis-Phillipe tried to fight them but took a fist in his belly, falling to the snow like Christ toppled from the cross.

Flat patches of black cloth dimpled on the periphery of her vision, and then abruptly the food dislodged. The splash and rattle of spoon in bowl sounded, as her hungry lungs drank air, rounds of coughing and gasps alternating. She hung her mouth over the sink, vision still patchy but coming back. The shiny silver crook of the spigot in her left hand's grasp reassured. For a time, Marcie cried in relief and gratitude, mashed bread floating in bowl-water like an abortion. Her fetus was probably that size now. She worried that her exertions against the sink edge had harmed it, then dismissed her worries as absurd.

When she could walk, she made her way to the living room and settled on the couch facing the windows, blinds drawn full up onto Rue Drummond, where a car scooped its headlights south and out of sight. She liked the feel of this apartment. The people made the place: both of them such friends and such flat-out attractive people. Marcie wondered if Travis had been at all serious about exploring a threesome, and she especially wondered what dear Laura's enigmatic look had meant. She didn't want to blow a great friendship, but maybe it could evolve into something very interesting indeed.

Across the street a woman went by carrying a sleeping child. From the blanket wrapped about it, one socked foot dangled, a wide patch of exposed skin between the sock and its rucked-up trouser cuff.

Minor alarms in Marcie's head. A mother oblivious to the situation could be unwittingly causing her child harm.

She rose, okay now, and went to the window, unlatching and lifting it wide enough to shout out, "Hello there!" trying that first, against an invasion of cold air, then, "Hello over there, your child's foot is uncovered!" She pointed, saw the woman turn, repeated what she'd yelled, hoping it carried.

The woman never broke stride—if anything, quickening her pace—but moved away as though engaged in kidnapping. Marcie gave it up and lowered the window, then the blinds, rubbing her hands. Only do so much, then you had to leave things to the fates or to other good Samaritans. Hmm, and speaking of children, it was probably time to look in on baby Jenny, just a peek in, a finger inside her sleepsuit, then gone.

Travis felt so strange as Swami Apadravya spoke, as if he were hearing forbidden wisdom: not the content so much as what strange breath it was riding on. The light greenhouse feel of satsang was with him as always, but as well there was a dark tinge to it, a flair of ginger-root concentrate teasing the corners of the air.

"In the Hindu tradition, holy men find control of the body a trivial matter. Sri Ramakrishna scorned to heal an illness he suffered, though he could easily have done so. He preferred to fix his mind on God rather than turn it to what he called this worthless cage of flesh. A yogi named Haridas had himself buried alive for six weeks, guarded by the skeptical, and came out of his hibernation unharmed in the presence of many witnesses. There are numerous other accounts, well documented, of the control of the physical body which comes with spiritual realization." Again came that dead silence of no-breath as he paused. The insuck, obscene and oddly enthralling. "Why do I relate all this to you? To what revelation are these arcane citations the necessary prologue?"

Startled upward. Broke the kiss: "It looks like the Angel is about to fall on us," she said.

Her boyfriend laughed. "Yes, and you make the earth move for me." But the statue's head jostled against wisps of cloud on black sky, and sharp screech of bronze protest on stone mixed with its swift stiff pivot and fall, a sick blast of cold on Huguette's face as the huge dark head fell with a meaty thud upon Louis-Phillipe's back. She heard a crack of bone, felt him press against her as if urged into the earth by a slab-hand. He swore from the pain, crying, a scared child. The square of the angel's base had stayed on its pedestal as though hinged on one side. A dark form wangled out from behind the squarish base, seemingly loath to show itself. Mute, muscular, all shadow as if a shamed retard. Had the dumb thing pushed the statue? But that'd have taken ten strong men. "Help us," she said, "please."

The shadow-head turned as if alerted to something. A crack like an icicle separating from an eave; then another more distant, then a series closer in, invisible houses in every direction letting ice crack and fall but never land. A vision came to her, pinned there: the sprung latches of meat lockers opening in the earth.

Then the stench came on, writhing in ravels along the snow, twisted lanyards of decay and rot. Two more bobbing heads joined their shy tormentor-savior, moved past him, a draw for him to follow; and then the moon lit them so that if Louis-Phillipe's crushing weight had not prevented her, she would have screamed. One found his left arm and arced it upward slowly so that Louis-Phillipe's coat wrinkled in elephant shift and his arm snapped free of its ball joint, skin tearing like an uncooked turkey leg but with blood in his cries; while it was still partway attached, the thing sank its teeth into his hand. Another knelt, grabbing her boyfriend's long hair so that his anguished face came away from her breast. The thing peered close at her, then the head craned to peer at Louis-Phillipe, and slowly it came in to sink a kiss deep into his cheek, tearing away flesh and beard like the marshmallow batting on a Sno-Ball; but what was exposed was not dark cake, but something wet and red, tongue fluttering in a shuddering mouth. Blood fell steaming on her, then cooled, chilling.

Sirens rose in the distance.

The two turned at the sound, mouths closed upon meat. Huguette could almost see the wheels turning: memory, the walking trove, a surround of life. They haltingly joined others, dark nightmarish shapes of stench staggering down the slope. Louis-Phillipe breathed his last. She tried to tug free, worried they might return or that other new-hatched monstrosities would pause to feed on her, but all her attempts came to nothing but pointless exertion. The winter air touched her, touched her, kept touching her.

"You have heard, perhaps, that I died, that by some miracle of resurrection I was restored to life."

My God, thought Travis, he's going to say it. It was one thing to see him up this close, a veneer of shockingly beautiful holiness animating his corpse as it maintained a mindful hold over a dynamo of mindless need behind; it was quite another to hear the man confess it aloud.

"I did not resurrect," Apadravya said, slight headbob like a dummy on a stick, eyes in useless blink. "Nor have I been restored to life." Laura's grip tightened and some tight fear let escape a far faint air-brake from her lips. "Those of you who have touched me understand. Those whose eyes are brought close know what I am: I died. I was put in the ground. I came out of the ground. I remain dead."

Anyone else had said such a thing, a ripple of laughs would have swept the hall. Instead, a brief murmur fanned the air, punched the gut of elation and left it foundering in dismay. Swami Apadravya did not lie—it had been alien to him in life; it was so now. Hackles stood at the back of Travis's neck, a feeling both harrowing and fulfilling.

"I am the first of many," he told them. "Others will come, and soon—others mired in samsara during their lives who will therefore be subject to unthinking appetites when they return. This eventuality cannot be prepared for, and yet you must prepare. Many in this room will be turned by them and will turn others. That is why I begin satsang in my beloved Montreal and carry it throughout this continent and beyond if I am able. It has not been given to me, the knowledge of *when* this upheaval will begin; but it will be soon, and I am here to witness and warn."

Travis was filled with dread. He'd seen a news photo once that had brought a similar horror: the close-up shot of a man's face, the caption saying that so-and-so watched helpless as his family and all his worldly goods burned up in the trapped inferno of his home. Travis flashed on his parents down in Florida, his brothers in Colorado and New York, Laura and Jenny and Marcie. What if it was starting right now? What if the streets were teeming right now, an army of corpses with the same thick hunger (but unchecked) he read now in Apadravya's eyes, pushing their way through his door, attacking Marcie and the baby?

Marcie reared back at the pungency of the stench, an oh-no sounding in her head: too close in the room, window shut tight, space heater roaring, and the sting of ammonia wrinkling the air.

Flooding the room with light, she rushed to the baby. No movement. No blinkback of brightness. Just stillness and a bloody froth coming from Jenny's nostrils and mouth. Panic rising, Marcie scooped up the lifeless child, sog to the sleepsuit, and hurried her to the changing table. A box of tissues, whip-whip-whip, three in her hand, wiping the froth away, gentle but quick. Then her mouth went to the baby's nose and mouth, grasping at vague CPR memories. A sour taste there. Think! What was different about CPR on an infant. You could blow out their lungs if you tried too hard. But how much was hard enough? Dead hand lay on baby Jenny's chest, its tiny fingernails tinged with blue. "Come on, come on," she pleaded, then back into mouth-to-mouth, preventing herself the luxury of sobbing, damage to the brain with each moment it missed oxygen, fingering the tiny cold palm.

Then came an abrupt clamp on her fingers. And before she could straighten to assess, the baby-head jerked up to her departing mouth and sank sudden ferret teeth deep into her lower lip, vicious and wild. The eyes were pooled and open and dead, but the teeth chewed and stung and the hand squeezed her fingers in a deathgrip and wouldn't be shaken loose. Her lip felt as if it had been snagged in a sewing machine gone out of control.

147

Behind her, a tremendous startle of shattering glass as she turned herself and her nemesis about to feel grave-stench and winter chill and to see (double disbelief, was she half-mad already and had she now gone completely over the edge?) what lurching horrors had ushered them in.

Marcie snapped on the overhead light and ran to the bassinet, an oh-no heating her thoughts as surely as the space heater was overheating the room. She'd read about Sudden Infant Death Syndrome a few years back, realizing now, with a why-didn't-I-see-it rising inside, how prime a candidate little Jenny had been.

Blinking back the brightness. Listless, sopping, but okay. Lifting her free of the miasma of ammonia, carrying her to the changing table, Marcie comforted, "There there, little Jenny. We'll get you out of these wet things, give you warm dry diapers, open the window a tiny bit, I don't care what crap your mommy gives me for it, you and me, we know what's best for baby, don't we?" The sleepsuit felt like an unwrung washcloth. She draped it over the wicker basket for non-stinky refuse, noting it would need a rinse in the kitchen sink when she was done here. Ruffle-soaked plastic pants joined them. Then the diaper, a damp runway of streaked brown as she unpinned and hourglassed it open: free it came, and she diaper-wiped the baby's bottom until it was clean enough for tickle cream; then a fresh new one efficiently pinned, and a t-shirt, and the green oversized sleepsuit, a lecture at once serious and funny bubbling in her head to deliver when Travis and Laura came home.

Behind her, the window gave a sharp rattle.

Travis was walking along cleared mounded sidewalks, the sound of sirens echoing one another from two distant parts of the city. It'd gotten to be too much—the dead holy man not ten feet away—and he'd mumbled some excuse to Laura, something about needing water. She'd be safe. He'd just pop home to reassure himself about baby Jenny and about Marcie, unspook himself from all this palaver about cemeteries disgorging their dead.

As he approached his building, he felt not a little foolish and decided that maybe the walk had been enough. He wouldn't disturb Marcie—or more to the point, he'd be damned if he'd give Marcie and Laura something to razz him about for weeks to come. But one peek through the window at baby Jenny sounded appealing. And the bathroom window was just this side of it: Maybe he'd catch Marcie, seized by an urge to luxuriate in a bubble bath, toweling herself off, her breasts bunched over terrycloth like buoyant pink balloons tipped with giving.

Dream on, he thought.

His boots were loud and scrunchy on the sanded press of snow underfoot, but he was halfway there and slowed to soften the noise. Odd. Jenny's room was bright. He came closer, saw the bassinet empty, saw Marcie at the changing table, solidly sveltely female, her red sheen of hair in a fetching chopcut that brought Tinkerbell to mind. Window was . . . hmm, yes it was, it was unlatched and *open*, the width of a swizzle stick. Christ, what an urge! What was the worst that could happen? He'd scare the shit out of her. She'd never speak to him again. She'd think he was one blasted dumbfuck and cool toward him from this moment on.

And the best? What the heck. He fingertipped under the sash. The window gave a rattle and Marcie turned her head. Game up. As he lifted the damned thing and slipped in, Marcie said, "Jesus, Travis, what are you up to?"

"Stay right where you are," he said, the authority of winter chill in his voice. "Keep changing the baby." He brought the window down all the way, latched it.

"Crazy fucker," she muttered. "Where's Laura?"

"Don't talk," he said, surprised at his boldness. He freed his hands, flopped his gloves like dead trout to the floor, undid his coat and stepped out of it. Coming right up to her, he set his left hand high on her hip and found, under her skirt with his right, the hot inside of her left leg just above the knee. No stockings. Firm warm flesh.

"You're insane." It was a whisper. There was a hint of admiration there, a turn-on.

149

"Shhh." Hand upward, soft muscled widening grippable inner thigh, Marcie not moving to stop him. Expecting the breechable barrier of panty elastic, he found sheer smooth undelineated flesh and then the moist archaic vulval pouch in lip-receptive mode. He thought of a one-handed unbelt, unclasp, unzip, a comical jog-dance behind her getting his pants and jockeys down past his dick. Uncool. Just a zip then, deft twist of the white cotton slit, up and over head and shaft, so he sprang out, zipper-teeth down by the balls like dead shark mouth. Up under her skirt like a silent-movie photographer, baby Jenny nonjudgmental over Marcie's shoulder, Marcie bending and widening to receive him, her ready vagina fisting him amazingly in, her bent-neck gasp as her hands knuckled protectively about his daughter.

Behind them, suddenly, the window exploded inward.

Baby's room smelled sweet if too close and warm. She felt along moonlight to the bassinet. Poor darling's lips weakly probed thumbward, her brow a wrinkle, then relax.

Marcie slowly zipped down the sleepsuit far enough to sneak fingers inside. Smooth plastic; beneath, still dry. Wonder baby, hundred-percent absorbent bladder and bowels. She hushed the zipper back upward, led the long red thumb back into the mouth where it stayed in renewed suck.

Too damned hot in here. She set the space heater two notches lower and the thing shut off. Then, yes, Laura be damned, she unlatched the window and tugged it open not so wide as a pencil. One more glance around the room and she headed for the door. The moment it closed behind her, the baby's forehead wrinkled sharply up. But her poop blurted out in great profusion and the tinkle flooded from her and her face eased into relieved sleep.

Travis was walking along cleared mounded sidewalks of snow one moment. The next, Laura was nudging him and the hall came back up around him. He was grateful, realizing he'd been simultaneously drawn into the dead guru's stare and impelled by revulsion into a desperate psychic escape, something involving Marcie and baby Jenny and a zip-gutted woman dragging her nude booted body over shards of jagged window glass to reach them.

"In life, there were many desires: Attentiveness and constant observation, appreciating them in their totality, in every articulated detail, led to their dying away. But in death, this death you see in me, there is but one clear and burning desire: to chew the red root of life in hopes that it will wake the palate, slide down the dead throat, revitalize the cold silent organs, and trick the walking shell of life into thickening inwardly even unto the cold core. As my words come forth, my witness is ever on that desire. There is no 'I' to control it, but only the fact of witnessing, the lifetime of making that my craft, which keeps me detached from that desire." Apadravya's teaching was, to Travis's astonishment, a strange mingle of comfort and terror. His thoughts went again to their child and to their upstairs neighbor.

But then, the auditorium doors let out a high squeal. Down the right aisle, people craning in their seats to see her, strode a woman, calling, "Rajib, save our son!" From under a knit cap, her short blond hair arched over a face of anguish. At her right shoulder, she held a slumbering child, blanket swaying as she came.

Huguette shivered fiercely under her dead boyfriend, a cold hoarseness in the throat she'd screamed silent. Warm numb tingling in her fingers and ears frightened her most, a first sign of frostbite setting in. She'd die here, the dark hump of the Black Angel's wingtops filling her vision and the incessant whine of sirens scouring her ears.

Then a miracle: Louis-Phillipe stirred.

No shuddered intake of breath, no pained groan at his mutilations. His intact cheek moved on her breast, stuck frozen in bloodpool, and she felt a surge of power stream through his body. "Louis-Phillipe?" she said, every sound but empty gasp gone. And then instead of lifting his eyes to her, his mouth found her nipple. Through the torn gape in his cheek, she saw him shred it, suffering the ravaging outrage of

151

pain even as she denied it. Rousing blood, his teeth mauled her. She tried to shove him away, but he was as unmoving as the statue—and yet, under her boyfriend's exertions, the Black Angel now bobbled. Zagging greedily down her body, he took huge bites as he went, and the top of the Angel's head gouged a raw furrow up his back. When he began scavenging the soft pit of her belly, the scandal of it put her into a merciful faint and then to death.

Louis-Phillipe's teeth furrowed lower.

"No, do not stop her."

The yoga instructor had risen to intercept her, had followed her onto the stage, but he backed away to sit in uncertainty, cross-legged on the stage edge, watching from a distance. Stepping onto the oriental rug, she unwrapped the blanket from about her son, letting him fall-flop into her arms. Only then, Travis saw, did the woman register what Apadravya had become. She flinched back, but almost immediately resumed her mission, the boy clearly not sleeping at all.

"Is he—?" Laura whispered.

Travis cut her off with a nod.

"This is my dear Aysha," said the guru. "And this is our son."

"He died this afternoon, Rajib." The woman's voice, unamplified and thrown upstage, only carried a few rows, but Travis and Laura were close enough to hear. "You can bring him back. You've been there. You have the power, I know you do."

"Oh my Aysha," said the holy man, and the way he said it touched Travis to the heart, "I have no such powers nor would I want them. He is well quit of the world. It were best he did not come back."

Travis saw a shaving of slush fall from her boot-heel onto the carpet. She swayed forward and laid the dead boy in the guru's lap. Then she knelt wordlessly, raising her hands in prayer.

Apadravya watched her. A sleeved left arm prevented the boy from twirling senselessly off his lap. He raised his right hand, training his attention on the child as his dead fingers rested on dead eyelids, thumb and pinkie upon the hinges of the boy's jawbone. The eyelids eased open. Travis saw that. Glisten of dark pupils, motionless and glazed. Then the swami's hand cupped to one side of the neck, and at once the small body convulsed violently, the nostrils flared and subsided, the limbs flexed. He came to as one sick and enfeebled, fixed on the dead eyes of his savior, whined for his mother, who crushed him in an embrace that seemed never ending. Sweep of murmur ran through the crowd.

And that's when the guru lost it entirely and leaped upon mother and child in a feeding frenzy so swift and so voracious it froze Travis and Laura in their seats even as it parabola'd them in hot freshets of blood.

Apadravya's dead fingers rested on the boy's face for what seemed an eternity. Then they came away, relaxed to a curve, as the holy man shook his head.

"I think I'm going to be sick," Laura warmed into her husband's ear. Not really, he thought. Just weirded out was all she was.

"Me too, hon," he said, but his eyes were riveted on the woman as she came forward and wept over the boy, still on the guru's lap. Compassion but not commiseration stood in the holy man's eyes, a light hand falling on his wife's shoulder.

Then it happened. At first, Travis thought it might be simple gravity, the turn of the boy's hand—or a brush past it by Apadravya's hand. But then it rose and gripped the woman's arm, and the boy's face was up and kissing his mother, her shuddering in amazement. And then they turned as, stumbling, she rose out of obscurity: There was blood between them, slick and new, her beige sweater red-icicled about the neck and her neck now below the ruin of her face a clutch-mouthed feast for her son.

The yoga teacher had risen and come forward, thinking clearly to separate them. But as soon as he laid his hand on the boy, it turned from its fallen mother and clung, an activated magnet, to *him*. Tar baby. He backpedaled. Too late. The bloodmasked dead boy was working its bloody way up the off-white cotton of his thigh.

Famished. An aching gape of hunger. Then, eyes in a scudded night opening. Dark lean-to. She peeled off from it, turning to rise, coat shrugged away and one thick numb gash bandoleered across her bloody front. Woozy thrumble, a catch on tombstone, neither cold nor hot at issue, but a hole into infinitude where her belly used to be. Mounded plots, spear-crunched under boot, slope gradual into black wink-gleam below. She led; she followed. A thing caromed against her, tumbled her groundward, scented her, stumbled on. She rose, followed sirens, lights, and a sear of cars scouring along Côte des Neiges. Down the mountain, down, down. Hunger flared. Her journey was long.

It happened so fast. He and Laura sat stunned, eyes on the besieged yoga instructor, who fell under the chomp of the dead boy onstage in a bloody heap. They didn't see his corpse-mother in one motion rise and fall upon the man sitting alone in the front row. His seat wrenched. Laura leaped up and Travis followed her leftward, shoving at the backs of those blocking the way: there was rude and there was necessary. Behind, the gutted yoga instructor rose to follow the toddler to the edge of the stage and over. The swami—one panicked look toward him sitting there with his legs crossed—was undergoing a titanic struggle and it was clear to Travis that his gentler side was losing. A woman screamed in the far aisle, and a high-pitched man shouted, "Keep your hands off mmmmrrrrh—!"

They gained the aisle. Travis glanced behind. The front-row guy was pulling himself up, bloody half-hands on his seatback. Red wattles drooped from one cheek. Jesus, why had they sat so near? The aisle ahead was jammed with panic: people shoved, fallen. To the right, a steel door with a bright red Emergency Exit sign, clogged with clever folks possessed by the same brilliant idea.

"This way," said Travis, gambling on the side stairs to

the stage. He shotgunned up them, reaching back a hand to Laura, pulling her free of the missed grasp of a newly risen ghoul. Ahead, the holy man was uncrossing his legs, a look of terrible conviction flaring upon his face. They veered left, past black hanging curtains, counting on some stage exit. Ropes and pulleys. A sound board. *There* it was, the way out. They took it. Stumbled down icy stairs into a dim-lit alley, Rue Mackay ahead if he was clear on where they were. They raced past dumpsters, light-pooled doorways, rounding northward out of the alley onto Mackay and straight into a moving crowd of hungry corpses, hands on Laura, hands on him, and then the cold crunch of teeth inevitable, biting deep.

Out the stage door, instinct shot his hand out to his wife. "What?" she said, frantic. "This way," said Travis and veered her rightward, down the alley away from Mackay, toward Bishop. Felt safer. Halfway in, past snow-crusted dumpsters, he glimpsed backward a mass of shamblers moving past the far alley-end. "Don't look back," he said, panic tight there, and Laura hunched her shoulders and quickened her pace to match his. Broke free of the alley's grasp, a clear breath on Bishop, then past the Musée des Beaux-Arts and scurrying along Sherbrooke, eyes sharp, past Montagne, one more block to Drummond—crazy as it was, if a taxi had come along, he'd have hailed it—turned north, home plate, their building in sight. A few blocks away, Travis heard a brake-squeal, impact of metal on metal, horns flaring up inside the confused weave of sirens that had followed them home.

A large man was heading south toward them, confusion in his walk. "He's too close," Laura said. "Run," Travis urged, and they did. He was poised to cut them off, blood glistening on his bald head. "Wait!" he shouted, a living man; "back there!" pointing in horror. "Sorry, can't help you. We'll call the police," Travis said, stunned that he and Laura kept walking, diagonaling across the dusted lawn to their apartment door. They might be dooming the sorry son-of-a-bitch. No matter. Couldn't get involved, no need for the inconvenience. Jesus, couldn't he tell they had their own problems? Anyway, Travis

155

really *would* call the cops, not that he expected they needed calling.

Closed the sucker out. He turned away from the front door, dismayed. "We should have—" Laura said and he told her he knew. He fumbled his keys, tried the wrong one, it was strange Marcie didn't come to the door, found it, gave it a turn, heard the click, and felt the knob wrenched out of his grasp from within.

His eyelids eased open. Travis saw that. Glisten of dark pupils, motionless and glazed. It amazed him, a dead toddler—for of that there could be no doubt—assuming the skin tone and motion and sleepy disorientation of a living breathing three-year-old.

Laura gasped beside him. "Let's get out of here."

"But why—?"

"I'll explain outside." She was already rising. The woman's face was wet with joy, her arms flung madly around her son. Apadravya sat quiet, corpse capable of miracles, danger hair-triggered beneath calm.

Travis followed Laura to the aisle, stupidly ducking as if to render his leaving invisible. When they had made their way to the vestibule, he asked her—buttoning up his coat as she hers—what the problem was.

"He's good," she said, hitting the doorbar and moving out onto Bishop, "he's very good."

"The swami?"

"He always *was* a mindfucker, but this is too much."

"What? The boy wasn't—?"

"It's why I lasted such a short time at the ashram." He did his best to keep up with her. Crossing Sherbrooke, he had to pull her back from stepping into the path of an advancing car. "He always seems so deeply holy, and never more so than tonight, even beneath that ridiculous makeup. But there's always trickery lurking. Aysha—or Sherri as she was known before he arrived—wasn't the only one. So wise, so warm, the man's a snake. Even now, he's a lure. I can see why I was drawn back tonight."

He fumbled a question.

"Almost. He almost had me. Bra undone. Exposed to him. But he let slip a look he thought I wouldn't see, a hunger. It was enough. I gathered up my things and left. Packed without telling anybody and knocked on my sister's door in the middle of the night."

Sirens whipped through the winter chill, but the bare night-time streets were magical and calm. "But Laura, I'm sure that kid was dead. How could a three-year-old—?"

"I don't know. Apadravya's hypnotic sometimes."

Travis recalled his mind wandering into fantasies of one sort or another as he listened. Maybe she was right.

"And dead is dead. It's not simply breathing, skin tone, the outward signs. There's brain damage involved. Organ damage. That child stood up there normal as could be. No, we were set up and I'm upset enough about it to call the cops. They could probably deport him on charges of drugging that little boy."

"I don't know what to think."

"He has that effect on people." Drummond at last. "Ah, home," she said. "Lovely Jenny. Lovely Marcie."

Brief surge of Marcie's face and form. "I love them too. You don't suppose that tonight we might . . . ?"

"Might what?"

"You know," he said. "What we talked about."

"Dirty old man. Now who's the Svengali?"

"Just say maybe, that's all, maybe."

The look Laura gave him was the type he wanted to pry off, it promised such sweets beneath the lidded tin of her eyes. "Maybe," she said coyly, and they were on their way up the walkway to the front door.

Wet thing cooled as Marcie munched, what she craved from it escaping through her teeth. Lost interest. She let the bunched bone-loose residue floop floorward.

Hint of sound back where she'd come from re-roused a need, same urgency, her bewilderment at the moist thing's inability to satisfy displaced by the monotonic pounding of I-want in her brain. She retraced her lurch out into brightness, hallway, food photos, crimson twin in mirror, key-jiggle at the door, turn, snick of deadbolt. Caught the slippery knob, crimped it, instinctual twist and tug, quick swing open: the meat, corpus animus, bi-fold. She hooked at heads, her hands thrilling to the warm vibrancy of neckmeat; but her grip held fast and the roaring faces came closer as her neck went sideways like a lover coming in for a kiss and she shoved them, despite a bonetooth of resistance, deep inside her mouth—two ripe breasts vying for the same insistent D-cup.

"Home early, I see." That smile. It made Travis's heart do backflips.

"You know how it goes," he said, following Laura's terse uh-huh inside. "A certain lovely lady got fed up with a certain guru's sleight of hand and—"

"And here we are," said Laura, paused with a hanger. "How was the little one?"

"Fine, fine. Slept all this time, not a whimper. I checked on her maybe half an hour ago. Dry as a bone."

Inside, he was feathers in wind. "How about a glass of wine and some conversation before you go?"

"Why not?"

"Let me get it," Laura offered, giving him a look he wished he could read. "White okay?" she asked, moving to the kitchen door, passing through it at their yeses.

Now, he thought, now. He considered coming up behind her, surprising her with a waistwrap. But she turned from the kitchen and there were those warm inviting eyes again. He held their gaze, opening to her as he approached, needs there yes, but also his naked integrity and his generosity toward her, his longing to comfort and embrace and incite her, to foment riots in her, to bubble her over and watch her glow and explode under his touch.

"What are you doing?" asked Marcie, and then her lips were there full and warm under his, and her amazingly lush body welled up beneath the press of textile. Peeling back off the kiss, he drifted to her ear, whispering there.

"You want me to?" she asked.

"She's ready."

"You're sure."

"Go on, you'll see."

She stepped away, stopped. "You'd better be right or you're dead meat," she said, then moved off.

"Don't I know it." Travis watched her go through the kitchen door. All he had, riding on this. Would she have the nerve to try? Or would they spar about one another as they pretended otherwise, chicken out, watch the evening's possibilities fade? It was awfully quiet in there. Corks not popping, no plash of wine on glass, no murmur of small talk, nothing. Outside, the window-dimmed keen of sirens; inside, the beating of his heart.

He closed on the kitchen door, went in, turning right around the leather-tan shine of the fridge. His chest was thick with dread and wonder. And there they stood, corked bottle forgotten on the counter, Laura's tight blond frame lovingly enfolded in Marcie's embrace. Familiar kisses in murmur there before him, his wife's yum-give-me-more under lips that still tingled at his.

Travis went to them, nice unhurried drift into female warmth that opened up to triangulate him. He kissed Laura long and deep, mirrored and modified it on Marcie's mouth; cupped buttocks—flank of filly and mare—as the two women shared the moist secrets he'd pressed into their lips.

"Let's go to the bedroom," he suggested, voice husky as heated flannel.

"Honey? Shouldn't we check on the baby?" Still shy, even now; and not a little woozy, as if the wine had found its way out of the bottle to her head.

"Not now," he assured. "Time enough later."

Then they moved off, riding the dream.

Aysha glowed, uncertain if she were awake or asleep. Rajib had concluded satsang quickly and she supposed she ought to feel guilt, but there was the fact of her living son, once dead and meatlike, now quick and warm, and Vish made all the rest of it inconsequential.

159

In the car, Rajib's young countryman driving, she had reached past Vish's thumbsuck to touch Rajib's hand. Ooze of warm unguent, tingling as if irradiated. "Stay with us tonight," she said, "with me and Vish." Rajib's awareness flitted over his eyes like a long-legged fly over stagnant pond-water. Then he spoke to his driver and Aysha offered directions.

She made tea, carrying the tray in to where Vish sat, thumb in mouth, staring at his father and nodding his head to any question. The tea lay untouched in its pot, steam from the thick spout dying down. Aysha walked Vish to his bed, tucked him in, kissed him, tore herself away with the greatest reluctance. Rajib sat precisely where she'd left him. She took his hand, clasped it palm to palm, pressing the dark back of it against her cheek—a faint sweet smell and a hint of foul. Four years rolled back. His goodness seemed ever daunting, but he had never stopped her—and he didn't do so now—from initiating intimacy. Aysha's knees dimpled the sofa cushion beside him. In the soft light of the oil lamp, he seemed almost alive.

His eyes tracked her. As she neared his face, slowly drifting in, she remembered how deep he got. Exponential. Asymptotic. But where once there had been joys unbearable and intense, orgasms of eye and nose to presage the sexual delights to come, now the joys were darkly tinged. In his gaze was the daunt of a hurricane eye. Upon his lips, she tasted bitter forbiddenness. She pressed deeper, his cool tongue flexing in familiar response as she probed. At the taut tease of his bite, micro-struggle at jaw-hinge, Aysha withdrew, rose, took his hand, led him to her bedroom.

Beneath the accordion-shuttered window, upon the slap and sploosh of their waterbed, Travis and Laura took their new beloved first. Marcie melted under their happy chore, her hands idling nicely upon strokable flesh as they found their lingual ways into her hot spots. She gushed and she swelled—and her release, a cataclysmic upheaval of seized and frenzied womanhood, delighted Travis to the depths.

Unlike Laura, who dishragged into limpness for a time after orgasm, Marcie tigered up supercharged from hers and dove for the sweet loins of his wife. Laura's giggle soon gave way to her yummy lip-gnawing sounds, woven with wind-howls from outside and the rattle of glass above. He gave her a deep kiss, asked her, mid-squinch, if she was having a good time, took her nostril-wheezy devour of a kiss as a positive response, and that then turned into an inhalation presaging the luff and buffet of her coming.

His ear teased him. He thought he heard the scrunch, slow and covered by woman-delight, of snow outside, almost as if someone were approaching the window. Then, shatters to scare the shit out of him, as the wood-slatted shutters angle-arced open over him like twinned jib-swings, booming right and left to let in a stinging spray of glass, abrupt waves of waspish pain carried in on unspeakable stench and winter cold. Marcie's back welled crimson under triangles of glass. Laura was screaming, trying to gain her balance on the waterbed, trying to cast off the cracked glaze that coated her torso. But then invader-stench hooked Travis's nose, and through the misted ache of his unblinded eye, he saw the jag-torso'd dead woman crawl through the window to lay claim to their lives.

Aysha undressed. She unwrapped her lover beside her bed, oil-lit dark skin oily and cool beneath her fingers, his clothing slick with savory-smelling unguent. Decades of hatha yoga had slimmed and toned his body, reminding her always, and especially now, of Jesus on the cross.

"I've missed you, Rajib," she said softly.

"It is good to be with you," came his reply.

She put her arms around him, standing there, and felt his hands lightly slat above the small of her back. White skin to brown, blond hair to black. Lovely naked embrace, full body. He was soft below where she remembered whippet hardness, thin sickle of dogtail roused. Her fondling did nothing. She fell to her knees, kissing a quiescent chest and abdomen, no breath there, just aromatic sheens of ooze like ancient spices preserving a corpse. Dark pubic wire. The small retired wrinkle of Rajib's penis. Aysha took it in like a second tongue, all of it, bathing it with saliva but to no avail. It had a subtle sweetness about it, like salt-sweet taffy, and the tip oozed drops of liquid manna, rolled like honeyed wine on her tongue before sliding down her throat.

"No blood," Rajib said, resting his hands on her bare shoulders. "No hardening. Lie down. And I will pleasure you."

She obeyed, settling on the cool blanket and watching the dark form of her husband part her thighs with bonelike steady hands, blessing her womanhood with his eyes. Lower he went, half on the bed, half off, until his lips touched her labia and his nose and forehead settled into a beloved pattern of duck and rise. She watched him as the feelings began, connecting with his eyes as in the old days, but in them, there cowered that dead thing she'd first noticed on the stage. It gleamed in oil-light. It thrilled, mingled there with his kindness. No breath on her yoni, no coming up for air, just movement and steady rise, soft sly tongue on her clitoris, then teeth, something new, upper teeth to lower trapping the wet nub, slick of cool tongue traveling to and fro, but the stiff enamel pressure crossed the line from pleasure to pain.

"No teeth," she said. He had taken her hands, as in the past, holding them at her sides, gentling her fingers.

Something sharp in his eyes. He eased off. His brow rose abruptly and she saw mustache and lip and teeth above the curl of her private hair. And then, like a rottweiler let loose, he lunged in and down. His hands closed on her hands, kept closing, crushing bone against bone. Bites of outrage ravaged her sex. Frantic with struggle, she tried her best to escape him, but it was useless: he was strong beyond mortal strength and his black locks flew hither and yon, all glistening with blood. Fear frenzied her, and in the midst of her frenzy she felt her bladder let go inside her red-runnered belly. A bloody gush of urine fountained against his face, awash over eyes which did not blink.

"No teeth," she said.

At once he eased off. Tongue again played slickly at her sex, its nub tip-tormented by tonguetip. Rajib's dead eyes shone a dark bloodlight of awareness across the heave and roll of her body. So tender did his corpse-hands move upon her palms and

162

fingers, and with such love, that Aysha felt his touch travel to her nipples, tighten them, a pure twin lick of love unstinting. Haloed shadows lapped in an array of grays on the ceiling glow, one barely substantial nimbus bobbing like a projection of Rajib's spirit. Focus rose to that nimbus, its rhythm, as each sensual wavecrash tumbled quicker upon the last, and again, and yet quicker, until there was nothing to do but yield up into the lovely god-glow with heart and mind and soul.

Feathering down, she gathered him up to lie upon her, naked brown corpse more caring than any living lover she'd ever had. His long dark locks tickled her shoulders. And though he slabbed upon her, no arhythmic answer to her in-out of breath, the dance of consciousness in his eyes made her cadaveric embrace all right, nothing freakish about it nor anything perverse: What, after all, animated *her* from moment to moment? And what distinguished her from him but breath and blood and rates of decay?

Outside, a siren screamed by. Its passing made Aysha aware of the distant weave of sirens in every direction, a thick blanket now, once tentative and threadbare.

"It's starting," he said, emotion unreadable as ever. "It seems that I have come too late."

She hugged him fiercely, suddenly afraid, wishing her touch could do for him what he had done for their son. In her dead lover's arms, she wept.

Their screams mingled, Marcie's and Laura's and his. Muffled flesh. Shoots of liquid falling everywhere. Arm and elbow flying, warm buttock, wet red hair matted about fingerfucked cuntmouth, hands hot and gone, waterbed slap under greenhouse coziness and the ecstatic shouts of love newborn. They settled down slowly, in a heap, a wild tea party, unPoppinsesque, bumping the ceiling in an ecstatic display of belly-laughter before parachuting downward.

Sirens whiffled in the distance.

"A restless night," said Laura.

"With any luck!" said Marcie, fruity alto laughter on the follow-up.

163

"Wow," offered Travis, mind-blown. "Wow, wow, double wow!"

"Articulate as always."

"Where have we been all our lives?" he wondered.

"Um," said Marcie, "on our way here?"

"I *guess*."

Laura surprised him: "I love you guys a whole heap."

"Same here." Gratitude in their neighbor's voice.

"And I love the fuck out of you two."

Quick Marcie: "As long as you also fuck the love out of us as frequently and as diligently as you can."

"Oh, Jesus in heaven, what have we here!" He thought then of the baby. "We ought to check on Jenny."

Laura groaned. "I guess I'd better. No need for you two to get out of bed."

"No, I mean I want all three of us to go." He warmed to the idea. "No clothing, just as we are, hugged through the apartment, shushing one another into Jenny's room, and peeking into the bassinet. I want to hold you close. I'd like to touch your beautiful naked flanks under moonlight, as Jenny sleeps below."

They grumbled, but they acquiesced.

The air in the baby's room was warm and close, but it concentrated his daughter's perfect smell and that was one virtue in it at least. She looked the perfect angel lying there.

Travis reared back at the pungency of the stench, an oh-no alarming in his head. "My baby," Laura gasped, then rushed in. Marcie followed and Travis came after, praying it wasn't what he feared.

Laura lifted the limp child in her arms, a wet bundle of laundry. Travis snapped on the overhead: no blinkback of light from the baby, not even a brief squeeze of closed eyelids. He saw the reddish froth at Jenny's nostrils and mouth. From the floor, the space heater roared obscenely.

"Quick," said Marcie. "The changing table." Box of tissues, whip-whip-whip, wiping the froth away, gentle but quick.

Then Laura's mouth came down upon her child's.

Travis felt helpless, paralyzed. Standing beside his wife, he steadied the baby's forehead, useless gesture but *something*. It was cold and dead. He saw the tiny fingers with their blue-tinged nails. His head swelled in the bad heat of the room.

Abruptly, near where his hands held dead temples, the baby's eyes flew open; and her mouth lit into Laura's face like a weasel-toothed hair-clipper plowing out of control, gone from his hands. Up her cheek the mouth pranced, path of red gouge gurgling Laura's screams. There by the table he and Marcie tried to wrestle her away, waltzing absurdly against the table edge as if it were crucial that they not drift too far from it.

Behind them, the window imploded jags of winter night upon them, an angled torrent of glass filling the air, and then, in plain sight behind his lovers, a young dead woman dragged herself over jagged shards, white red-zipped torso snagging there but coming on anyway, bringing in hordes of stenched dead in her wake. His dead infant unlatched from Laura and dove for him like screaming hell, the bright air no barrier to its bloody-mouthed leap.

What the fuck is happening here, was the thought that spun in his brain as the side of his face lit up, what the fucking blue blazes is happening here?

Perfection. Things had come together just as he had hoped they would. Jenny, sleeping peacefully below in her bassinet, held a lifetime's promise beneath those precious eyelids. After ages of lust for his upstairs neighbor, he had enjoyed her and found her overwhelmingly more sensuous than his most detailed jag-fant of her. And there wasn't, no not in the slightest, an iota of jealousy—if anything, he found an amazingly complementary desire—in Laura.

A snap at Jenny's window. He veered his head.

"What, silly?" Laura said.

"That sound startled me." A tracery of white webbing made the pane appear fractured.

"Just sub-zero stuff."

165

But he unhugged them and crossed the warm rug and off on cold floorboards in the moonlit room, peering out upon the smooth blue drifts in the alley, the windowless brick facade over yonder. Utter peace. Marcie, drifting behind him, swept to his left, gentling a hand on his shoulder, a thigh hot against his thigh. "What's out there?"

"Not a thing, sweet love. Just deep freeze and a lot of sleeping souls." Even the sirens had stopped.

Laura joined them, her hands like tickling lilies at their waists, her hip-lyre at their buttocks. Saying not a word, she kissed his left shoulder and rested her cheek there, hairfall a new tickle. Travis, replete with peace and contentment, raised a hand to the window, benedictive gesture, felt the wall of cold air an inch away, touched a palmpress to the surface frost, drew away. Marvelous, how thin the barrier was between unsurvivability and a perfect moment. He was grateful, beyond gratitude, to be standing on this side of that barrier, safe, loved, an heir to such bounty as he'd never known could exist on this earth.

It happened when he kissed Marcie's cheek. A sudden insuck of breath, the pulling tight of soft flat belly at his right palm where it lay above her Brillo-flare of red private hair. He swerved up to look, caught a glimpse of blue-puffed flesh, but was buffeted by the cold coming in on a shatter of glass, nothing there, a flicker of dream, everything there, too sudden the assault, the rag-wrapped gnarled knuckles smashing through triangling glass to lay claim to his life. Flat pane onto empty alley. A flying mass of forced shards and the influx of stench and bodies and hands and mouths coming in too fast to react to. His wife reaching under his cleft to brush against his balls, feeling his prick stiffen in response. The insuck of air filled with slashes of glass and a naked woman—scored at torso like a zipper of guts—diving in to kiss a visegrip chaw deep into his turned cheek. "Let's go back to bed," Marcie wantoned into his ear, as, giddying upon a peak of ecstasy, he gazed at a zigzag of bricks over yonder. His legs failed him under the flying assault of his attacker, her arms impossibly strong, her face fastened to his where it bit and tore. Beneath his attempts to scream, his eyes caught Laura, pinned under a half-formed male monstrosity, whose huge meaty hand boned into her breast and ripped it up and away like a flesh balloon filled with pudding, its mouth its goal as Laura screamed and resisted him without effect. Baby Jenny gave a tiny cry of protest, then fell silent, and Travis shared a smile with his lovers. "She's okay, I think," he said, "and I bet the three of us could find something nice to do in the other room." A vision of hunger flickered at the window, nothing, the startle of an eyeblink, emptiness out there. "Help me," Marcie shouted, but he couldn't turn and a winterfall of cold air and meat gone way bad assaulted his senses as hands gripped one leg and raised it up to a mouth, and a dead tongue brushed the toes of his other foot. Not a sound outside. The sharded air screamed with sirens, police and ambulance, firetrucks and air attack, a doomsday medley of wails at each other's throats in a threnody of pain. The women dropped to their knees, backed Travis's butt onto the cold sill, mouthed at his shaft with teasing warm wet lips and tongue, while his shoulderblades touched and shied away from the flat frosty pane of glass. Smash to either side and a give as if it'd been open all this time, tumbling backward, then yanked by brute force through and back into an alley full of subway-packed shuffling forms. They tugged him down onto the rug and one impaled herself on him while the other pussied at his face, Laura's taste, and from above came the sounds of kissing as Marcie pistoned about his penis, and his tongue did a new-angled, newfangled dance at clit and labia. The woman bit and tore mercilessly at his jaw, and the pain of teeth closing on foot and thigh lit up his head and forced his muscles to the straining point. But then a shambleman loomed up and arrowed down into his belly, a clutch there like food poisoning cramping him up, but from the outside. And it got worse and worse, not subsiding for a breather, but attacking deeper and with pain unending. Laura came, burrowing and rocking at his mouth so that for a spell he couldn't breathe, but then he maneuvered his nose in time for Marcie's climax—Laura having fingered her clit

167

where he and Marcie groined together—and he shot his seed deep into her, his moans muted by the wet luff of Laura's cunt. He died there on that rug, red bleed on gray, grave-soiled tufts of fabric. They collapsed upon him, laughing at the freeing licentiousness of their hearts, doubled femininity asquirm where it most mattered. Rising, swim of the room into his ken, he watched Laura feeding the baby to Marcie and the others. Its bawling had torn free of siren scowl, but now ripped down into stillness. He kissed their hands and whispered "I love you" into Marcie's then Laura's ear, then left Jenny's room with them, softly closing the door while blowing his sleeping girl a kiss. Bladder and bowel gave way then in the overheated room, but it would be four hours too late before the door again opened. And he went, ravenous, for the smashed window, dragging himself across the shards of glass, watching indifferently one arm slice open like dark gristled meat detaching from chicken wing, lunging away from the window-shattered warmth and on into the unending hunger of a long winter's night.

ABOUT THE AUTHOR

ROBERT DEVEREAUX made his professional debut in Pulphouse Magazine in the late 1980's, attended the 1990 Clarion West Writers Workshop, and soon placed stories in such major venues as Crank!, Weird Tales, and Dennis Etchison's anthology MetaHorror. Two of his stories made the final ballot for the Bram Stoker and World Fantasy Awards.

His novels include Slaughterhouse High, A Flight of Storks and Angels, Deadweight, Walking Wounded, Caliban, Santa Steps Out, and Santa Claus Conquers the Homophobes.

Robert has a well-deserved reputation as an author who pushes every envelope, though he would claim, with a stage actor's assurance, that as long as one's writing illuminates characters in all their kinks, quirks, kindnesses, and extremes, the imagination must be free to explore nasty places as well as nice, or what's the point?

Robert lives in sunny northern Colorado with the delightful Victoria, making up stuff that tickles his fancy and, he hopes, those of his readers.

You can find him online at Facebook or at www.robertdevereaux.com.

deadite press

"Brain Cheese Buffet" Edward Lee - collecting nine of Lee's most sought after tales of violence and body fluids. Featuring the Stoker nominated "Mr. Torso," the legendary gross-out piece "The Dritiphilist," the notorious "The McCrath Model SS40-C, Series S," and six more stories to test your gag reflex.
"Edward Lee's writing is fast and mean as a chain saw revved to full-tilt boogie."
- Jack Ketchum

"Bullet Through Your Face" Edward Lee - No writer is more extreme, perverted, or gross than Edward Lee. His world is one of psychopathic redneck rapists, sex addicted demons, and semen stealing aliens. Brace yourself, the king of splatterspunk is guaranteed to shock, offend, and make you laugh until you vomit.
"Lee pulls no punches."
- Fangoria

"Zombies and Shit" Carlton Mellick III - *Battle Royale* meets *Return of the Living Dead* in this post-apocalyptic action adventure. Twenty people wake to find themselves in a boarded-up building in the middle of the zombie wasteland. They soon realize they have been chosen as contestants on a popular reality show called Zombie Survival. Each contestant is given a backpack of supplies and a unique weapon. Their goal: be the first to make it through the zombie-plagued city to the pick-up zone alive. A campy, trashy, punk rock gore fest.

"Slaughterhouse High" Robert Devereaux - It's prom night in the Demented States of America. A place where schools are built with secret passageways, rebellious teens get zippers installed in their mouths and genitals, and once a year one couple is slaughtered and the bits of their bodies are kept as souvenirs. But something's gone terribly wrong when the secret killer starts claiming a far higher body count than usual . . .
"A major talent!" - Poppy Z. Brite

"The Book of a Thousand Sins" Wrath James White - Welcome to a world of Zombie nymphomaniacs, psychopathic deities, voodoo surgery, and murderous priests. Where mutilation sex clubs are in vogue and torture machines are sex toys. No one makes it out alive – not even God himself.
"If Wrath James White doesn't make you cringe, you must be riding in the wrong end of a hearse."
-Jack Ketchum

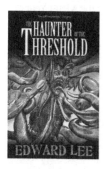

"The Haunter of the Threshold" Edward Lee - There is something very wrong with this backwater town. Suicide notes, magic gems, and haunted cabins await her. Plus the woods are filled with monsters, both human and otherworldly. And then there are the horrible tentacles . . . Soon Hazel is thrown into a battle for her life that will test her sanity and sex drive. The sequel to H.P. Lovecraft's The Haunter of the Dark is Edward Lee's most pornographic novel to date!

"Apeshit" Carlton Mellick III - Friday the 13th meets Visitor Q. Six hipster teens go to a cabin in the woods inhabited by a deformed killer. An incredibly fucked-up parody of B-horror movies with a bizarro slant
"The new gold standard in unstoppable fetus-fucking killfreakomania . . . Genuine all-meat hardcore horror meets unadulterated Bizarro brainwarp strangeness. The results are beyond jaw-dropping, and fill me with pure, unforgivable joy." - John Skipp

"Super Fetus" Adam Pepper - Try to abort this fetus and he'll kick your ass!
"The story of a self-aware fetus whose morally bankrupt mother is desperately trying to abort him. This darkly humorous novella will surely appall and upset a sizable percentage of people who read it . . . In-your-face, allegorical social commentary."
- BarnesandNoble.com

THE VERY BEST IN CULT HORROR

deadite
press

"Rock and Roll Reform School Zombies" Bryan Smith - Sex, Death, and Heavy Metal! The Southern Illinois Music Reeducation Center specializes in "de-metaling" – a treatment to cure teens of their metal loving, devil worshiping ways. A program that subjects its prisoners to sexual abuse, torture, and brain-washing. But tonight things get much worse. Tonight the flesh-eating zombies come . . . *Rock and Roll Reform School Zombies* is Bryan Smith's tribute to "Return of the Living Dead" and "The Decline of Western Civilization Part 2: the Metal Years."

"Necro Sex Machine" Andre Duza - America post apocalypse...a toxic wasteland populated by bloodthristy scavengers, mutated animals, and roving bands of organized militias wing for control of civilized society's leftovers. Housed in small settlements that pepper the wasteland, the survivors of the third world war struggle to rebuild amidst the scourge of sickness and disease and the constant threat of attack from the horrors that roam beyond their borders. But something much worse has risen from the toxic fog.

"Whargoul" Dave Brockie - It is a beast born in bullets and shrapnel, feeding off of pain, misery, and hard drugs. Cursed to wander the Earth without the hope of death, it is reborn again and again to spread the gospel of hate, abuse, and genocide. But what if it's not the only monster out there? What if there's something worse? From Dave Brockie, the twisted genius behind GWAR, comes a novel about the darkest days of the twentieth century.

"The Vegan Revolution . . . with Zombies" David Agranoff - Thanks to a new miracle drug the cute little pig no longer feels a thing as she is led to the slaughter. The only problem? Once the drug enters the food supply anyone who eats it is infected. From fast food burgers to free-range organic eggs, eating animal products turns people into shambling brain-dead zombies – not even vegetarians are safe! *"A perfect blend of horror, humor and animal activism."*
  - Gina Ranalli

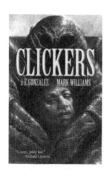

"Clickers" J. F. Gonzalez and Mark Williams- They are the Clickers, giant venomous blood-thirsty crabs from the depths of the sea. The only warning to their rampage of dismemberment and death is the terrible clicking of their claws. But these monsters aren't merely here to ravage and pillage. They are being driven onto land by fear. Something is hunting the Clickers. Something ancient and without mercy. *Clickers* is J. F. Gonzalez and Mark Williams' gore-soaked cult classic tribute to the giant monster B-movies of yesteryear.

"The Innswich Horror" Edward Lee - In July, 1939, antiquarian and H.P. Lovecraft aficionado, Foster Morley, takes a scenic bus tour through northern Massachusetts and finds Innswich Point. There far too many similarities between this fishing village and the fictional town of Love-craft's masterpiece, The Shadow Over Innsmouth. Join splatter king Edward Lee for a private tour of Innswich Point - a town founded on perversion, torture, and abominations from the sea.

"Urban Gothic" Brian Keene - When their car broke down in a dangerous inner-city neighborhood, Kerri and her friends thought they would find shelter inside an old, dark row home. They thought they would be safe there until help arrived. They were wrong. The residents who live down in the cellar and the tunnels beneath the city are far more dangerous than the streets outside, and they have a very special way of dealing with trespassers. Trapped in a world of darkness, populated by obscene abominations, they will have to fight back if they ever want to see the sun again.

"Jack's Magic Beans" Brian Keene - It happens in a split-second. One moment, customers are happily shopping in the Save-A-Lot grocery store. The next instant, they are transformed into bloodthirsty psychotics, interested only in slaughtering one another and committing unimaginably atrocious and frenzied acts of violent depravity. Deadite Press is proud to bring one of Brian Keene's bleakest and most violent novellas back into print once more. This edition also includes four bonus short stories:

AVAILABLE FROM AMAZON.COM

CPSIA information can be obtained at www.ICGtesting.com
Printed in the USA
BVOW08s1040250814

364131BV00016B/248/P